"We'll get along even if it kills us."

To Lucy's horror she heard herself say, "You mean you'll actually be nice to me?"

"I've never in my life met a woman as contentious as you! Don't you ever let up?"

"I wouldn't be so cranky if you'd act like a human being," she retorted. "It's because you're so—so unreachable."

"Unreachable is exactly what I am, and what I intend to remain," Troy answered grimly. "And don't, if you value living, ask why."

Dear Reader,

Welcome to the first of three scintillating books by Sandra Field. When Sandra first came up with the idea for *Beyond Reach* she fell in love with her characters so much that she couldn't bear the thought of leaving them behind. So she wrote another book. And then another....

"This series of three books crept up on me unawares. After Troy and Lucy met in the West Indies, I found myself curious to discover how marriage would change them. Hence *Second Honeymoon*, again set on an island, this time off the coast of Nova Scotia. Lucy's laid-back friend Quentin and her uptight sister Marcia played minor roles in *Second Honeymoon*. Once Quentin had appeared on the scene, I knew I wouldn't rest until I'd brought him face-to-face with Marcia, which I did in my next book, *After Hours*."

Follow Lucy and Troy's continuing story in *Second Honeymoon*, out in August 1996. Marcia and Quentin's own romance appears in *After Hours*—coming in early 1997 in Harlequin Presents!

With warm wishes,

The Editor

SANDRA FIELD

Beyond Reach

Harlequin Books

TORONTO • NEW YORK • LONDON
AMSTERDAM • PARIS • SYDNEY • HAMBURG
STOCKHOLM • ATHENS • TOKYO • MILAN
MADRID • WARSAW • BUDAPEST • AUCKLAND

ISBN 0-373-11806-6

BEYOND REACH

First North American Publication 1996.

Copyright © 1995 by Sandra Field.

CHAPTER ONE

LUCY BARNES stared at the words on the board as if she was mesmerized, as if someone was offering her precisely what she wanted most of all in the world.

The individual letters were printed forcefully on a square of white cardboard with an indelible black marker. A masculine hand, she'd be willing to bet, Lucy thought with a distant part of her mind, and read the notice again.

> Wanted. Cook/crew-member for four weeks, starting immediately, on chartered 50-foot sloop. Maximum four guests. Apply at *Seawind*.

She raised her head, looking past the bulletin-board where the notice was pinned to the sunlit row of yachts moored along the cement dock. Several of them were sloops. Which one was *Seawind*? As if in response to her question, the wind from the sea lifted her hair, teasing its long mahogany-colored curls against her neck. The trade winds, she thought in pure excitement. The famous trade winds of the West Indies that she had read about in geography class, when she had been a little girl and had thought the whole world open to her... But that she had waited until now to experience. She could sail out of this harbor under their impetus. Sail among the green-clad volcanic islands that rose from a sea so blue that it made her feel like shouting for joy. She took two impetuous steps toward the dock.

5

And then she stopped. Think, Lucy. Think, she ordered herself. You've already landed yourself in one mess by acting on impulse. A royal mess. One that you're not finished with yet. Are you going to compound it by taking another leap into the unknown without considering all the consequences? Let's face it. An hour ago all you wanted to do was get on the first plane out of here and head home. Where at least you know the rules, even if you don't like them very much. Chewing her lip, she stood indecisively, the sun beating down on her face and arms, her flowered skirt blowing against her legs like a sail luffing in the wind.

How she wanted to be on that boat! Four weeks of sailing among the Virgin Islands. Four *weeks* . . .

Lucy thrust her hands in the pockets of her skirt, looking around her. On the other side of the road that led into the marina there was a wooden bench under a tree adorned with fat clusters of orange flowers. An oleander hedge flanked the road, its sharp-pointed leaves rustling gently, its salmon-pink blooms bobbing up and down. So much color, so much beauty . . . Lucy marched across the road and sat down, and knew even as she did so that this way she could see if anyone else came along to read the notice and try for the job on *Seawind*.

The slats of the bench were hard under her thighs. The dappled shade of the tree played with the flowers on her skirt. Tame flowers, she thought absently, running her fingernail along the stem of a tidy little rose. Northern flowers. Nothing like the exuberant blossoms of Road Town, capital of Tortola, largest of the British Virgin Islands. Where she, Lucille Elizabeth Barnes, now found herself.

Her money-belt dug into her waist. At least she still had that. Her money, her return ticket and her passport. Even if that was all she had. Her luggage was sitting in the guest bedroom of the villa belonging to Raymond Blogden, who had been—very briefly—her employer. And there it was likely to stay until she went back with reinforcements. Large male reinforcements. Because she wasn't going back alone, that was for sure.

Her two sisters had thought she was crazy to answer the advertisement in the Ottawa paper, while her cool, commonsensical mother had said, 'But what about the clientele you've worked so hard to build up, Lucy? Surely if you leave for a month—especially after you've just been ill for three weeks—some of them will look elsewhere? Had you thought of that?'

But the ad—rather like the printed notice on the bulletin-board across the road—had seemed like a message from heaven.

Family vacationing in British Virgin Islands requires a massage therapist for month of April. Excellent salary and comfortable quarters in hillside villa in Tortola.

The ad had been placed in March, when winter had been at its worst in Ottawa. Dirty snowbanks edging all the streets. Gray, overcast skies. Not a blossom to be seen anywhere... only the dull, dispirited green of pine and spruce trees that had been battered by frigid winds since December. No wonder she had jumped at the chance of warmth and color and sunshine! To top it all off, she'd been ill for nearly a month, miserably ill, with a flu virus that had clung to her as tenaciously as the patches of ice had clung to the front steps of her apartment building. She had craved a change of scene, a break in her routine. Something different and exciting.

Her lips twisted wryly. Well, she'd certainly gotten that. Rather more than she'd bargained for. Shutting from her mind the ugly little scene that had been played out in the spacious hallway of the hillside villa, she firmed her mouth and tried hard to think in a manner of which her elder sister Marcia would approve.

She could go to the police station, explain what a fool she'd made of herself, trust that they would help her get her luggage back and then head for the airport. Her return fare, luckily, was an open ticket, prepaid by Mr Blogden. She could fly out on the first available seat and go back to Ottawa. Because her mother was right. She, Lucy, had worked extremely hard over the last four years to build her reputation and steady list of clients, and it was irresponsible of her to jeopardize everything she had struggled so long to establish.

She got up. The police station was only a few blocks away. The worst part would be the explanation of why she had fled the Blogden villa at high noon minus her luggage. After that, she'd be home free.

She should go home. Of course she should. Even though she'd finally paid off the last of her student debts, she had her eye on a little house in the country outside Ottawa. If she was going to take on a mortgage she had to do everything in her power to ensure a regular income.

She didn't want to live in the city for the rest of her life. Her good friend Sally thought she should stay there so she'd meet more men; the countryside was devoid of eligible males, according to Sally. But, for now, Lucy was through with men. Big blond men who weren't there when she needed them. The only kind she ever seemed to be attracted to.

A woman in a colorful sarong skirt was approaching the bench. Lucy collected her wandering thoughts; this wasn't the time or the place to deal with her problems with the opposite sex. Perhaps this woman could direct her to the police station.

Then, from the corner of her eye, Lucy saw a flock of gulls rise in the sky over the moored yachts. She stood still, her gaze following the graceful curves they were inscribing against the depthless blue of the heavens, where the rays of the sun made the flashing white wings translucent. Their cries were like the cackling of a coven of witches, mocking her decision. Making nonsense of it.

Responsible. Sensible. Should. Ought. Horrible words, Lucy thought blankly. Words that had ruled her life for as long as she could remember.

The woman in the sarong skirt had already walked past her. In sheer panic Lucy made a small gesture with her hand, as though to call her back. Then her hand fell to her side. Feeling her heart pounding in her chest, she knew that somehow she had made a decision. A momentous decision. She wasn't going back. She was going to walk down the dock and find *Seawind* and do her level best to get herself signed on as cook and crew.

Rubbing her damp palms down her skirt, she fastened the image of the gulls in her mind's eye like a talisman and crossed the road. The sign was still there, its black letters every bit as forceful as she remembered them. There was an urgency behind the words, she decided thoughtfully. Whoever had written them was desperate. Good. All the more chance that he'd hire her. That she'd have four weeks at sea. Four weeks to figure out why the job she'd worked so hard to create had swallowed her up in the process. Four weeks to try and understand why she was always drawn to the wrong kind of men— handsome, blond, sexy, undependable men.

Four weeks to have fun?

She suddenly found that she was smiling. Taking a deep breath, Lucy marched down the dock.

She passed *Lady Jane*, *Wanderer*, *Marliese* and *Trident*. Then she stopped in her tacks, feeling her heart leap in her ribcage. *Seawind* was painted white with dark green trim, her furled headsail edged in green, the bimini awning over the cockpit a matching green. She was beautiful. Wonderfully and utterly beautiful.

'Can I help you?'

Lucy jumped. A bemused smile still on her face, she turned to face the man who had seemingly appeared from nowhere. He was standing on the dock four or five feet away from her, wearing a faded blue T-shirt and navy shorts. For a moment, knocked off balance, Lucy thought she must have conjured him up out of her imagination, for he was big, blond, handsome and sexy— exactly the kind of man who had become anathema to her over the last few months. The kind she was intent on avoiding at any cost. 'Oh, no. No, thanks,' she said. 'I'm looking for the skipper of *Seawind* actually.'

'Are you applying for the job?'

None of your business, thought Lucy. 'Yes, I am.' With a sudden clutch of dismay she said, 'It's not filled, is it?'

'No. What are your qualifications?'

'I think I should leave that for the skipper, don't you?' she said sweetly.

'I'm *Seawind's* skipper.'

Then why didn't you say so in the first place? Lucy thought crossly. And why in heaven's name did you have to be big and blond and overpoweringly masculine? Smothering the words before she could speak them, she held out her hand with her most professional smile. 'I'm Lucy Barnes.'

His grip was strong, his own smile perfunctory. 'Troy Donovan. Tell me your qualifications.'

He had every right to ask; he was, after all, the skipper. She said calmly, 'Would you mind if we went on board? I'm not used to the sun and I'm not wearing any sunscreen.' Her sunscreen, along with everything else, was back at the villa.

After a fractional hesitation he said, 'Go ahead.'

She stepped from the dock to the transom of the boat called *Seawind*, and without being asked slipped her feet out of her sandals before stepping on to the teak deck. The bimini cast a big square of shade. The wood was warm and smooth under her bare soles. She had to get this job, Lucy thought, determination coursing along her veins. She had to. Waiting until Troy Donovan had positioned himself across from her, she said, 'For nearly four years, as a teenager, I spent all my free time sailing. Daysailers, Lasers, and then as crew on a forty-five foot sloop not unlike this in design.'

He said edgily, 'Would you mind taking off your sunglasses? I like to see the person I'm talking to.'

She pushed her glasses up into her hair. Her eyes were her best feature—thick-lashed and set under brows like dark wings. Beautifully shaped eyes, that hovered between gray and blue and bore tiny rust flecks that echoed the rich, polished brown of her hair. Her face had character rather than conventional prettiness: her chin pointed but firm, her nose with a slight imperious hook to it. To the discerning eye it was a face hinting at inner conflicts, for, while her lips were soft and her smile warm, a guardedness in her eyes hinted that she might withhold more than she gave.

Troy Donovan said abruptly, 'How old are you now?'

'Twenty-five.'

'Haven't you sailed since then?'

Unerringly he had found her weakest point. 'No—I've lived in Ottawa for many years. But I've never forgotten anything I learned, I know I haven't.'

'Where did you do your sailing?'

'Canada. Out of Vancouver.'

'So you don't know these waters at all?'

She tilted her chin. 'I can read charts, and I'm a quick learner.'

'Can you cook?'

Although one of Lucy's favorite haunts was the Chinese take-out across the street from her apartment building, her theory had always been that if you could read, you could cook. Somehow she didn't think that particular theory would impress Troy Donovan. But her mother had always taught her that you could do anything you put your mind to, and not even several flunked physics exams and a failed engagement had entirely destroyed Lucy's faith in this maxim. With a nasty sensation that none of her answers were the right ones, she said evasively, 'I haven't actually cooked on a boat before. But I'm sure the same general principles hold true at sea as on land.'

'What about references?'

His eyes, too, were gray. But unlike hers they were a flat, unrevealing gray, like the slate from the quarry near her old home on the west coast. With a sinking heart she said, 'I'm self-employed. But I can put you in touch with the bank manager where I do all my business dealings, and my physician would give you a personal reference.'

He looked patently unimpressed. 'You can come back tomorrow, Miss Barnes. If I haven't found anyone by then, perhaps I'll reconsider you.'

He was dismissing her. He wasn't interested. She was going to lose out on something that she craved more than breath itself. Lucy said in a rush, 'I don't think you quite understand—I love the sea! I come alive on a boat that's under full sail. I'd give everything I own for four weeks on the water...*please*.'

He had been standing with one hand wrapped around the backstay. Straightening, he ran his fingers through his hair and said, exasperated, 'I've got enough on my mind without taking on someone who's never sailed here before. I'm sorry, Miss——'

'I'll do it for nothing,' she blurted. 'Food and board, that's all.'

'Are you in trouble with the law?' he said sharply.

'No!' Her brain racing, she sought for words to convince him. 'Haven't you ever wanted anything so desperately that you'd sell your soul to get it? You don't really know why—you only know that your whole body is telling you what you want. That you're denying yourself if you ignore it.'

So quickly that she almost missed it, a flash of intense emotion crossed the carved impassivity of his features. He, like her, had pushed his sunglasses to the top of his head, where they rested in hair that was a thick, sunstreaked blond. While Lucy was something of an expert in body language and the long term effects of tension, she didn't need her expertise to realize that Troy Donovan had been under a severe stress of some kind for far too long: the toll was clearly to be seen in his shadowed, deepset eyes, his clenched jaw, the hard set of his shoulders.

He didn't answer her question. Instead he said slowly, 'So you're desperate... Why are you desperate, Lucy Barnes?'

'I—I can't tell you that. I'm not sure I know myself. But I'll work my fingers to the bone and I'll do my very best to please your guests. And I'm certainly strong enough physically for the job.'

His eyes ranged her face with clinical detachment. 'You don't look strong. You look washed out. In fact,' he continued, with almost diabolical accuracy, 'you look as though you're not fully recuperated from some sort of illness.'

Damn the man! He'd found every chink in her armor. Worse than that, by telling him how much she wanted the job she'd revealed to him a part of herself that she would have much preferred to keep private. 'I've had the flu,' she replied shortly, and with reckless disregard for the frown on his face plunged on, 'Why don't you take me out for a trial run? So I can prove I'm the right person to crew for you.'

'Give me one good reason why I should bother doing that.'

She had nothing to lose and everything to gain. Her nails digging into her palms, Lucy said with false insouciance, 'Your notice said you needed someone immediately.' She looked around and gave him an innocent smile. 'And I don't exactly see a huge line-up of other applicants.'

As his facial muscles tightened she felt a thrill of primitive victory. He said flatly, 'The trouble is, it's too early for college students, and anyone else who's half reliable has long ago been snapped up by the big charter companies.' He added, his gray eyes inimical, 'Let's get something straight, Miss Barnes. I'm the skipper, you're the crew. I give the orders and you take them. Is that clear?'

Refusing to drop her own eyes, Lucy said, 'Those are the rules on board, yes.'

'Didn't you bring a pair of shorts with you?'

A blush crept up her face. 'No. I—no.'

'Check in the forward cabin—the drawer under the port bunk. You can borrow a pair of mine.'

In spite of herself her voice shook. 'You mean you'll take me for a trial run?'

'Yeah...that's what I mean.'

She gave him a dazzling smile that lit up her face and gave her, fleetingly, a true beauty. 'Thanks,' she said breathlessly. 'You won't regret it.'

Before he could change his mind, she climbed up on the foredeck, her bare feet gripping the roughened fiberglass. The forward hatch was open. With the agility of the fifteen-year-old she had once been, she climbed down the wooden ladder into his cabin. It had two bunks, one unmade; a faint, indefinable scent of clean male skin and aftershave teased her nostrils. Closing her mind to it, as she had closed her mind to the awkward truth that once again she was doing her utmost to involve herself with a big, handsome, blond man, Lucy pulled open the left-hand drawer. She scrabbled among Troy Donovan's clothes, not quite able to ignore how intimate an act this was, and shook out the smallest of the three pairs of shorts there. Dropping her skirt on the bunk, she pulled them on. They might be the smallest pair, but they were still far too big, the waist gaping, the cuffs down to her knees. After grabbing a canvas belt coiled neatly in the corner of the drawer, she cinched in the waistband and let her T-shirt fall over it.

She looked ridiculous. And somehow she wasn't so sure that that was a bad thing.

Not stopping to analyze this, Lucy climbed back on deck. A skipper from another boat had ambled over to help with the mooring lines. Troy said, giving Lucy's attire a single derisive glance, 'The ignition switch is by the radio. Then you can retrieve the anchor—these are the handsignals I'll use.' Briefly he demonstrated them.

'We'll head out under power, and once we're in the strait you can hoist the mainsail.'

She should have been nervous. But, as the diesel engine began to throb beneath her feet, Lucy felt such a purity of happiness rocket through her body that there was no room for anything else. Again she went forward, pulling on the gloves she found stowed by the anchor winch and glancing back over her shoulder to catch all Troy's instructions.

The groaning of the winch and the clanking of the anchor chain made her feel fully alive, every nerve alert, every muscle taut. As she guided the chain into its berth she found herself remembering for the first time in many years how at fifteen she had anticipated in hectic detail the way such feelings might be deliciously enhanced by that mysterious act called making love.

How wrong she'd been! Big blond men. Bah! The next time she fell in love, Lucy decided, it was going to be with someone short and stout and bald. Then *Seawind* began to move, and all her concerns, her love-life included, vanished from her mind.

Within minutes she'd hauled in the fenders and stowed them away. The dock was receding. The channel with its red and green buoys beckoned them on. Troy said, 'There's sunscreen in the cupboard under the bar. You'd better put some on before we get out on open water.'

Again Lucy went down the companionway steps. The cabin was spacious, constructed from highly polished mahogany. Two couches, flanking a dining table inlaid with marble, two padded swivel chairs, a chart cupboard and a neatly appointed galley were all fitted in without any sense of constriction, and again Lucy felt that shaft of unreasoning happiness. As she smoothed the cream over her face and arms the deck began to lift and fall beneath her feet.

When she want back up, Troy said tersely, 'You can hoist the mainsail now.'

She fastened the halyard to the headboard and began hauling on the sheet, bending her knees to give herself leverage, using every bit of her strength. Following Troy's instructions, she tightened the winch, slotting the handle and bracing herself against the companionway. Then she unfurled the headsail and trimmed it to a port tack. The breeze had freshened as they left the confines of Road Harbor. Troy turned off the engine and suddenly *Seawind* came to life, her bow rising and falling as she heeled into the wind that was her reason for being.

'Isn't this wonderful?' Lucy cried, giving Troy another of those brilliant smiles that held nothing in it of seduction yet was infinitely seductive.

Her shirt was molded to her body, her hair whipping about her ears. 'Ease off the headsail,' he ordered in a clipped voice.

Lucy knew enough to do as she was told. But, spoiling her exultation, a cold core of dismay had appeared somewhere in the vicinity of her gut. Did she want to sail with a skipper who so plainly hated his job? He had yet to give her anything approaching a real smile. Even now, as he checked the masthead fly and adjusted the wheel, he didn't look the least bit happy to be out on the water.

'We'll change tacks in a few minutes,' he called. 'I'll tell you when.'

This maneuver went without a hitch. Then Lucy took a stint at the wheel, delighted to find that her old intuitive sense of wind and sail had never left her. After they'd changed tacks again, Troy questioned her on the rules of the road and threw a number of hypothetical situations at her to see how she'd deal with them. Then they headed back to the harbor, running before the wind.

Finally, Lucy furled the headsail and folded the mainsail on the boom, and before she knew it Troy was backing into the dock. He was, she had to admit, a more than competent skipper.

The engine died, and into the silence Lucy said tautly, 'Do I pass?'

He leaned against the folding table that ran along the centre of the cockpit and answered her question with another. 'It's ten or eleven years since you sailed, right?'

'Ten.'

'You loved it.'

'They were the best years of my life,' Lucy heard herself say, and felt her face stiffen with shock as the truth of her words struck home. 'That's nuts, isn't it?' she said, more to herself than to him. 'It can't be true...'

'It sure doesn't say much for anything that's happened since then.'

'No...' she whispered. 'It doesn't.'

Ruthlessly Troy Donovan hurled two more questions at her. Are you married—or living with someone?'

'No and no.' Fighting to regain control of herself—what was it about this cold, unfriendly man that made her reveal herself so blatantly and so unwisely?—she added, 'Are you?'

'I'm interviewing you, not the reverse,' he retorted. 'If you're independent, and you so clearly love sailing, why aren't you living on the west coast again?'

'Mr Donovan,' Lucy said coldly, 'this is a hiring session. Not a counseling session.'

'The name's Troy. Why don't you answer the question?'

'Because I can't!' she flared. 'Because the reasons I live where I do are nothing to do with you. *I'm* not asking *you* why you never smile, why you have a job that you seem to dislike so thoroughly. Because it's none of my business.' Her face changed. 'Please...are you going to hire me?'

'I don't have much choice, do I?' he said unpleasantly. 'The first guests come on board the day after tomorrow and there's a pile of work to do in the meantime. However, I won't make you do it for nothing.' He named a salary that was more than fair. 'I want you to take my vehicle now, and go to the grocery——'

'You've hired me—for four whole weeks!' Lucy interrupted. 'But that's terrific! Oh, I'm so excited!' Grabbing the extra fabric that flapped around her slender legs and holding it out like a skirt, she did a solemn little dance on the deck. Then she gave him a wide grin. 'I'll do the very best I can, I promise.'

Because Troy was standing in the shade he had pushed his sunglasses up again and there was in the flint-gray eyes an unquestionable, if reluctant, smile. Much encouraged, Lucy said pertly, 'So you do know how to smile. You'd be extremely handsome if you smiled properly, you know.' She bared her teeth in an exaggerated smirk. 'You should try it some time.'

'Lucy,' he said tightly, 'maybe now's as good a time as any to make something else clear. You and I are going to be living and working together in pretty close quarters for the next month. There'll be no male-female stuff between us—have you got that?'

His smile was gone as if it had never been, and the anger that she'd already sensed as a huge part of his make-up was very much in evidence. She stared right back at him. 'You're afraid I might make a pass at you?'

Biting off the words, he said, 'Of course I'm not afraid of you! But the comfort and security of the guests is our only concern for the next four weeks. You and I are co-workers—and that's all.'

She could match his anger with an anger of her own—it would be all too easy—or she could keep her sense of humor. Choosing the latter—because his pronouncement definitely had its funny side—Lucy gave a hoot of laughter. 'No problem! Now if you were five-feet-seven, bald and overweight, then you should worry. But tall, blond and handsome—nope. I'm immune. Thank you very much.'

'I don't see what's so funny,' he snarled.

'I don't think you see anything very much as funny,' Lucy said, with more truth than tact. 'And I swear that's the last remark of a personal nature that'll cross my lips today.'

He said—and Lucy was one hundred percent sure he hadn't meant to say it, 'Immunity implies exposure.'

'Indeed,' she said drily. 'I fell in love with my first blond hunk—the history teacher in school—when I was twelve, and I've been doing it ever since. When I came down here, I'd made a vow—no more blond men. Bald is beautiful. So you're quite safe, Troy Donovan. Now, what was that about groceries?'

'For their sakes, I'm glad none of them married you,' he said nastily.

Lucy flinched. She would have married Phil, who'd had wavy blond curls and had proposed to her among the tulips along the Rideau Canal when she was twenty-three years old. But Phil had met Sarah, chic, fragile Sarah, two months before the wedding, and had gone to Paris with Sarah instead of staying home and marrying Lucy. She said, almost steadily, 'If they had I wouldn't be crewing for you, would I? What did happen to your previous cook, by the way?'

'Her son crushed several bones in his foot last night. She flew to San Juan with him this morning.' His scowl deepened. 'I shouldn't have said that about marriage—I'm sorry.'

Despite her vow, a vow she fully intended to keep, Lucy was already aware that it would be much safer if she disliked Troy. He was taller than Phil, more handsome than the history teacher, and sexier by far than anyone she had ever met. 'Grocery store,' she repeated in a stony voice.

'I'll give you the keys to my Jeep. I want you to cook supper for me tonight, as if I were a guest—an appetizer to go with drinks, then dinner and dessert. This evening you can draw up menus for the next six days and I'll check them over. Our first charter is just one couple, Craig and Heather Merritt, from New York. They'll come on board the day after tomorrow—by then you've got to have the boat provisioned and spanking clean brass and woodwork polished, bathrooms spotless, beds made so they can have their choice of cabin. I'll look after ice, water supplies and the bar, and in the meantime I'll overhaul the engine and the pumps. Any questions?'

She blinked. 'No. But some time today I'll have to get my suitcase.'

'Use the Jeep,' he said impatiently.

It was by now blindingly obvious to Lucy that Troy didn't like her at all and wouldn't have hired her if he'd had any other options. In fact, he thought so little of her that he considered her unmarried state a boon to the male sex. So she might as well confirm him in his dislike; it would beat going to the police. She said in a small voice, 'I need to borrow you as well as the Jeep.'

He frowned. 'Surely you haven't got that many clothes? Storage space is limited on a boat, as you should know.'

Lucy said rapidly, 'I arrived in Tortola this morning, planning to work for a family with a villa in the hills.

But when I got to the villa it very soon became plain that the family wasn't about to materialize and that the man of the house and I had radically different ideas about the terms of my employment.'

'He put the make on you?'

She grimaced. 'Yes. So I left with more haste than grace via the nearest window, and my suitcase is still there.' Her shoulders slumped. 'I'm scared to go back there alone,' she confessed. 'But I could go to the police if you don't want to go with me, Troy. It's nothing to do with you, I do see that.'

'I'll go,' Troy said with a ferocious smile. 'This has been the week from hell, and I don't see much chance of it improving—I could do with a little action. Why don't we go there first?'

Lucy took a step backwards and said with absolute truth, 'I'm not so sure that you don't frighten me more than Raymond Blogden.'

'I almost hope he resists,' Troy said, flexing both fists. The muscles of his forearms moved smoothly and powerfully under his tanned skin and there was such pent up energy behind his words that Lucy backed off another step, until the teak edge of the bench was hard against the backs of her knees. 'I know nothing whatsoever about you,' she muttered, 'and yet I've agreed to live on a fifty-foot boat with you for a month. Maybe *I* should be asking *you* for references.'

'You can always check with my bank manager and my physician,' he said with another fiendish smile. 'Anyway, if nothing you've done since you were fifteen has impressed you as much as sailing a Laser, you might benefit from throwing caution to the wind. Let's go.'

It was, Lucy thought, not bad advice.

And throwing caution to the winds had brought her to Tortola in the first place, hadn't it?

CHAPTER TWO

LUCY hurried below, changed back into her skirt, and five minutes later was driving west out of Road Town. Troy drove the Jeep as competently as he drove a boat; she couldn't help noticing that the muscles in his thighs were every bit as impressive as those in his arms, and forcibly reminded herself of her vow. Fortunately, in her opinion, to be truly sexy a man had to be able to laugh...

They braked for a herd of goats trotting along the road, and then for a speed bump. 'The turnoff's not far from here,' Lucy said, her pulses quickening.

The driveway to the villa wound up the hill in a series of hairpin turns; all too clearly she remembered running down them, glancing back over her shoulder in fear of pursuit. It seemed like another lifetime, another woman, so much had happened since then. And then the Spanish-style stucco villa came in sight and her heart gave an uneasy lurch. It looked very peaceful, the bougain-villaea hanging in fuchsia clouds over the stone wall, the blinds drawn against the glare of the sun.

Troy drew up in front of the door and pocketed his keys. 'Why don't you stay here?'

She had an obscure need to confront Raymond Blogden again. 'I know where the case is,' she murmured, and slid to the ground.

Troy pushed the doorbell.

The chimes rang deep in the house. A bee buzzed past Lucy's ear, and from the breadfruit trees behind the house a dove cooed monotonously. Troy leaned hard on

23

the bell, and from inside a man's voice said irritably, 'Hold on, I'm on my way.'

Lucy recognized the voice all too well, and unconsciously moved a little closer to Troy. The door swung open, Troy stepped inside without being asked and Lucy, perforce, followed. 'What the——? Who are you?' Raymond Blogden blustered. 'Get out of my——' And then he caught sight of Lucy. His recovery was instant. 'Well, well... I'm glad you came back, Miss Barnes,' he sneered. 'I was about to call the police. Breach of contract and destruction of personal property should cover it, don't you think?'

He was a big man, his black hair slicked back in the heat, his expensive white linen suit dealing as best it could with a figure whose musculature had long ago been subsumed by fat. Rings flashed on his fingers. Lucy remembered how they had dug into her arm and shivered.

Troy said with icy precision, 'I wouldn't do that if I were you, Mr Blogden—you should be thankful Miss Barnes isn't at the police station charging you with assault... Go get your case, Lucy. You're quite safe this time.'

The house was shaded and cool and very quiet. Lucy scurried down the hall to the bedroom that was to have been hers, finding her blue duffel bag exactly where she had left it on the tiled floor. She picked it up and ran back to the foyer. Raymond Blogden's complexion was several shades redder than when she had left. 'Perhaps you wouldn't mind telling me your name, young man?' he was saying, and to her horror Lucy saw his right hand inching toward his pocket.

'Troy, he's got a weapon!' she cried.

In a blur of movement Troy went on the offensive. Three seconds later Raymond Blogden's arm was twisted behind his back and Troy was saying calmly, 'Search his pocket, would you, Lucy?'

As gingerly as if a tarantula inhabited Raymond Blogden's pocket, Lucy inserted her fingers and came up with a pearl-handled knife that was disconcertingly heavy. 'We'll take that,' Troy said cheerfully. 'And since I'm rather fussy about those with whom I associate, Mr Blogden, I think I'll keep my name to myself.'

'She's nothing but a hooker,' Raymond Blogden spat. 'She dresses it up with fancy words, but that's all she is.'

'Shut up,' Troy said, very softly, 'or I'll have your hide for a car seat... Ready, Lucy?'

She was more than ready. She opened the door and heard Troy say, in a voice all the more effective for its lack of emphasis, 'If I ever see you within fifty feet of Miss Barnes again, I'll wipe the floor with that pretty white suit of yours... Goodbye, Mr Blogden.'

The sunlight almost blinded Lucy. Troy gunned the motor and surged down the driveway. He was whistling between his teeth and looked extremely pleased with himself. 'You enjoyed that,' Lucy said shakily.

'Damn right I did.' With casual skill he took the first of the turns. 'What in heaven's name made you think you could work for a man like that?'

'I never met him,' she said defensively. 'The interview was in Toronto, with his personnel adviser.'

'And what do you do that led him to call you a prostitute?'

'I'm a massage therapist,' she said. 'There are certain people who seem to think that massage has everything to do with sex and nothing to do with healing—I get so tired of all the innuendoes and off-color jokes.'

'It's a very useful profession,' Troy said mildly.

She shot him a suspicious glance. 'Do you really mean that?'

'Kindly don't equate me with the likes of that creep up in the villa!'

Only wanting to change the subject, Lucy looked distastefully at the knife in her lap. 'What am I going to do with this?'

'Keep it. In case you're ever silly enough to work for someone like him again. Naïveté doesn't pay in any job, but particularly not in yours, I would have thought.'

Troy had spoken with a casual contempt that cut Lucy to the quick. I won't cry, she thought, I won't. If I didn't cry when it happened, why would I cry now?

But the hibiscus blooms that bordered the driveway were running together in big red blobs, as red as Raymond Blogden's face. She stared fiercely out of the side window of the Jeep and felt Troy slow to a halt as they reached the highway. Then his hand touched her bare elbow. 'Don't!' she muttered, and yanked it away.

'Look at me, Lucy.'

'No!'

'Lucy...' His fingers closed on her shoulder.

She turned to face him, her eyes brimming with fury and unshed tears, her mouth a mutinous line. 'You're only the skipper when you're on the boat,' she choked. 'Let go of me!'

If anything, his hold tightened. Lines of tension scoring his cheeks, his gray eyes bleak, he said, 'I owe you another apology, don't I? You'll have to forgive me, I'm—out of touch with the female sex. You did well to get away from him; he's as nasty a piece of work as I've come across in a long time.'

A tear dripped from her lashes to fall on his wrist. 'I—I was so f-frightened.'

'Of course you were, and rightly so. That charming little object in your lap is a switchblade.' As she regarded it with horror, Troy asked, 'How *did* you get away from him?'

'He has a collection of jade in the hallway. I picked two pieces up and told him I'd drop them if he didn't stay where he was. I g-guess he didn't believe me. So I dropped one on the floor and it s-smashed. I felt terrible, but I didn't know what else to do.' She gave a faint giggle. 'You should have seen the look on his face. He said he'd paid nine thousand five hundred and forty dollars for it. Once I'd climbed out the window I put the other piece on the sill and ran for my life.'

The look on Troy's face was one she hadn't seen before. Admiration had mingled with laughter, and with something else she couldn't name but that sent a shiver along her nerves. She said fretfully, 'Let's get out of here—I want to go back to *Seawind*.'

Troy checked for traffic and turned left. 'The supermarket's going to be an anticlimax after this.'

Knowing her lack of culinary skills, Lucy wasn't so sure that he was right. Although wrestling with menus would certainly beat wrestling with Raymond Blogden. 'I need to blow my nose,' she mumbled.

Troy fumbled in the pocket of his shorts and produced a small wad of tissues. He checked them out, then said, grinning at her, 'No engine grease—I thing they're okay.'

It would be a great deal safer to dislike Troy Donovan, Lucy thought, swiping at her wet cheeks then burying her nose in the tissues and blowing hard. When he grinned like that it not only took years off his age, it put his sexual quotient right up there with Robert Redford's. She blew again, reminding herself that violence was what had put the grin there in the first place.

A physical confrontation with another man. She'd do well to remember that.

She put the tissues in her skirt pocket and said, before she could lose her nerve, 'Thank you for going with me, Troy. I was dreading having to explain the whole situation to the police.'

'You're entirely welcome,' he replied. 'Haven't had as much fun in months.'

'You'd have made a good pirate,' she snapped.

'Blondbeard?' he hazarded.

Smothering a smile, she went on severely, 'You *like* violence?'

'Come on, Lucy—that was a situation straight out of a Walt Disney movie. He was the bad guy, I was the good guy coming to the rescue of the beautiful maiden, and because I was bigger than him and, I flatter myself, in better condition, right triumphed. How often in these days of moral ambiguities do we have the chance to participate in something so straightforward?'

She frowned. 'You haven't answered the question, and I don't think the grin on your face is quite as easily explained as all that.'

'Of course it's not,' he said shortly. 'Mind your own business.'

So she wasn't to be told why Troy hadn't had as much fun in months. And his tone of voice had pushed her away as decisively as if he'd strong-armed her.

Women must be after him in droves, she thought, her lips compressed. So, didn't he like women? Certainly he hadn't answered her when she'd asked if he was married or living with someone.

All her warning signals came on alert. Keep your distance. So what if he's a handsome blond? You know your weakness for them and you're not going to fall into that trap again. You're not!

But the sunlight through the windshield was glancing on the blond hair on Troy's arms, shadowing the hollow in the crook of his elbow where the veins stood out blue, and his fingers gripped the wheel with an unsettling combination of sensitivity and strength. Lucy remembered the speed with which he'd pinioned Raymond Blogden's arm behind his back, the strength with which he'd almost lifted the other man off the floor.

The knight in shining armor. The villain. And she herself cast as the beautiful maiden.

A hackneyed story. But—she knew from the languorous throb of blood through her veins—a primitive and still powerful story, nevertheless.

She'd better bring her mind back to the menus. She could handle *Seawind*; she had no fears on that score. But meals for several days for four people, one of them the steel-eyed Troy Donovan? Now that was a challenge.

Not nearly the challenge of keeping her distance from that same steel-eyed Troy Donovan.

An hour later, after paying ten dollars for a driver's license, and having been given Troy's account number at the supermarket and strict instructions to drive on the left, Lucy was on her own. All she had to do was get the supplies for tonight's dinner and come up with ideas for the next few days.

That was all, she thought wryly, standing in front of the meat counter and wishing she'd paid more attention in her grade nine home economics classes. But home economics had taken third place to sailing and the captain of the basketball team: six feet tall, blond and—by the not very demanding standards of a fourteen-year-old—incredibly sexy.

Tom Bentham. Who'd dated her, Lucy, twice and then gone steady for the next two years with petite and pretty Tanya Holiday.

Someone jostled her and Lucy brought her mind back to the present with a bump. She roamed the store, cudgeling her brain for some of her mother's recipes. Her mother combined a career as a forensic pathologist with a reputation as one of the city's most elegant hostesses, whereas Lucy's idea of fun on a Saturday night was a group of friends, a case of beer and pizza ordered from the neighborhood Italian restaurant.

She began putting things in the cart. The couple from New York no doubt had very sophisticated tastes, and Troy, she'd be willing to bet, was on a par with them. A man didn't acquire the kind of confidence he wore like a second skin by doing nothing but chartering yachts in Tortola. She'd got to impress him. She didn't think he'd fire her—he needed her too much for that—but he could make life very unpleasant for her if he chose.

Another forty-five minutes had passed before she was lugging the brown paper bags of food on board. Troy, stripped to the waist, his hands coated with grease, had the various components of a pump spread over the table in the cockpit. He gave her a preoccupied nod as she eased past him. 'I ran the engine while you were gone— so the refrigerator's cold.'

'Thanks,' she said, and disappeared into the cabin as fast as she could. His image had burned into her brain: the dent in his chin, the entrancing hollow of his collarbone, the tangled blond hair on his deep chest. It's not fair, she thought wildly. No man should look that gorgeous.

Not only gorgeous, but oblivious to his own appeal. Because Troy, she was quite sure, wasn't trying to impress her with his physique. Troy was merely oiling the pump and didn't want to get his shirt dirty.

He wasn't interested in her enough to try and impress her.

Scowling, Lucy stepped down into the galley. It was past six o'clock already. She'd better get moving. She'd decided to make a crab and cream cheese dip, chicken Wellington, a sweet potato casserole, broccoli with a hollandaise sauce, and a chocolate fondue with fruit. All of these were tried and true recipes of her mother's that she herself had made at least once. She'd mix the pastry first and put it in the refrigerator to set, then do the two sauces and get the dip in the oven.

An hour later Troy came down the stairs, shrugging into his shirt. 'How're you doing? I'm getting hungry.'

The hollandaise sauce had curdled, so she'd had to resuscitate it in the blender; she'd forgotten to get cream for the chocolate sauce and every inch of counterspace was cluttered with dirty dishes and partially cooked food. 'Fine,' she said, trying to look cool and collected when she could feel the heat scorching her cheeks and wisps of damp hair clinging to her neck.

'I wouldn't want the guests seeing the galley in such a mess,' he commented.

'Troy,' Lucy snapped, 'I haven't figured out where everything is yet, I've had a long and difficult day, and chaos is a sign of creativity. Didn't you know that?'

The anger that was so integral to him flared in response. 'Chaos can also be a sign of disorganization. Didn't *you* know *that*?'

It had been a more than difficult day, and Lucy suddenly realized she was spoiling for a fight. Making a valiant effort to control her temper, she said, 'The crab dip will be done in fifteen minutes, and I'll serve it to you in the cockpit.'

'I'm serious, Lucy... People come on these cruises to relax, to get away from it all. The state the galley's in is totally unacceptable.'

She should count to ten. She should smile politely and ask him if he'd like a drink. Lucy banged a saucepan on the plastic counter and cried, 'You may be the skipper—but I'm the cook! The galley's *my* territory. Not yours. I'd appreciate your keeping that in mind.'

He leaned forward, his voice honed to an edge as deadly as the pearl-handled switchblade. 'Don't think I'm so desperate for crew that I can't fire you.'

'Go ahead!' she stormed. 'I dare you.'

Her eyes, fueled by rage, were the turbulent blue of the sea under gray skies. In her free hand she was clutching a butcher-knife she'd been using to chop onions; her breast was heaving under her blue knit shirt, her whole body taut with defiance.

Troy said scathingly, 'You're behaving like a ten-year-old.'

'At least I'm capable of emotion!'

'Just what do you mean by that?'

'I mean you're as cold as the refrigerator. You're frozen, solid as the block of ice in the——'

A man's voice floated down the companionway. 'Ahoy, *Seawind* ... Anyone on board?'

Troy's muttered profanity made Lucy blink. He said furiously, 'Don't think we're through with this—because we're not. I'm the boss on this boat, Lucy, and you'd better remember it.' Then he turned on his heel and took the steps two at a time. She heard a stranger's jovial laugh and then the murmur of masculine conversation.

For two cents she'd follow Troy up those steps, march down the dock and leave him in the lurch. Let him find another crew-member! What did she care? One of the reasons she'd become self-employed was so she wouldn't have to deal with dictatorial male bosses. Because one thing was clear to her: what she had earlier labeled as Troy's confidence wasn't confidence at all. It was arrogance. Downright arrogance.

High-handedness. Despotism. Tyranny.

The buzzer rang on the stove. The crab dip was as perfectly browned as any her mother had ever made, and smelled delicious. Balancing it on top of one of the gas elements on the stove, Lucy heaved a heavy sigh. Tyrant though Troy was, she still wanted to sail out of the harbor the day after tomorrow. She wanted to hear the slap of waves under the prow and feel the helm quiver with responsiveness. She wanted to swim in the turquoise waters of a coral reef...

She reached for the packages of crackers she'd bought, and five minutes later was climbing the steps with a platter on which the crackers and some celery stalks were artistically arranged around the dip. 'Hello,' she said, with a friendly smile at the man sitting across from Troy.

'Jack Nevil,' he said bluffly, getting to his feet. 'Skipper of *Lady Jane*... Is this for us? You've lucked out, Troy.'

Lucy smothered a smile. Troy said with a dryness that wasn't lost on her, 'I sure have... Want a beer, Jack? Or something stronger?'

'A beer'd be great... and one for the lady?'

'The name's Lucy,' she said limpidly. 'I'd love one; it's been pretty hot in the galley.'

Her eyes, wide with innocence, met Troy's. He was quite aware of her double meaning, she saw with some satisfaction. He said blandly, 'Jack, who was that chemist who won the Nobel prize—Prigogine? His thesis was that at a state of maximum disequilibrium, a system will spontaneously create its own order—I think that's Lucy's theory of cooking.'

'If this dip is anything to go by, the theory works,' Jack said enthusiastically. 'Have a seat, Lucy.'

'Oh, no,' she said sweetly, 'I'd better get back to work. Troy's a hard taskmaster.'

'Only that I have a preference for eating before midnight,' Troy responded equally amiably. 'Thanks, Lucy...see you later.'

And who had won that round? Lucy wondered as she went back to the steaming-hot galley. If she were an optimist she could call it a tie.

But Jack Nevil and her mother's crab dip had probably saved her from being fired.

Two hours later Lucy twirled the last strawberry in the chocolate sauce and took another sip of the German dessert wine in her glass. She'd drunk rather more wine than was good for her in the course of the meal. Maybe to hide the fact that Troy had spoken very little as they ate. Or maybe so she'd have the strength to face all the dirty dishes stashed below. 'What a glorious night,' she said soulfully.

Jack had left before dinner, having demolished the crab dip and three beers. She and Troy were eating on deck, where the smooth black water was illumined by a three-quarter moon and stars glimmered in the blackness overhead. It was blissfully, blessedly cool.

'That was an excellent meal, Lucy,' Troy said brusquely. 'But entirely too elaborate—I can't have you spending all day in the galley when you'll be needed out on deck.'

She took a gulp of wine. 'Is that what's called damning with faint praise?' she said provocatively.

His eye-sockets were sunk in shadow, his irises reflecting the harbor's obsidian surface. 'And that's another thing,' he said, in the same hard voice. 'You and I can fight like a couple of tomcats from sun-up till sundown tomorrow. But when the Merritts come on board there'll be no more fighting. We'll get along even if it kills us.'

To her horror she heard herself say, 'You mean you'll actually be nice to me?'

He banged his clenched fist so hard on the table that the cutlery jumped. 'I've never in my life met a woman as contentious as you! Don't you ever let up?'

'I wouldn't be so cranky if you'd act like a human being,' she retorted. 'It's because you're so—so unreachable.'

'Unreachable is exactly what I am, and what I intend to remain,' he answered grimly. 'I said no male-female stuff and I meant it. And don't, if you value living, ask why.'

Any flip reply Lucy might have made died on her lips, because there was genuine pain underlying Troy's voice and the moonlight lay cold along his tightly held jaw and compressed lips. He had a beautiful mouth, she thought unwillingly. Strongly carved yet with the potential for tenderness. What had made him so unreachable? Had filled him to the brim with suppressed rage?

Whatever it was, it was his secret. Nothing to do with her.

Swallowing the strange bitterness this conclusion caused her, Lucy let her thoughts march on. There was more than an element of truth in everything Troy had said. The meal *had* been too elaborate. And people didn't pay high rates for a charter to spend their time listening to the crew fight all day. She downed the last of her wine and said forthrightly, 'I'll prepare simpler meals from now on. And I'll do my best not to lose my temper again.' She gave him a small smile. 'Or at least not more than once a day.'

His mouth softened infinitesimally. 'I should have told you there's a very good delicatessen on one of the backstreets—you can buy a lot of stuff already prepared and freeze it. Quite a lot of it's West Indian style, so the guests enjoy it. Plus, it would make life much easier for you.'

'Oh. That's a good idea.' And because Troy's voice, like his face, had gentled, and because she was alone on the deck of a yacht in the tropics by moonlight with a handsome blond man, she babbled, 'I'm going to give the galley a good cleaning tomorrow before I bring in the supplies. The brass lamps and fittings are tarnished, so I'll polish them, and then I'll——'

'It's okay, Lucy... If there's one thing I've learned today it's that you're a hard worker. Why don't you go to bed now? You must be exhausted. You can take one of the cabins downstairs and I'll sleep up at the bow.'

'I think you just gave me a compliment,' Lucy said dazedly. 'A real one.'

'I believe I did. Off you go.'

Struggling to collect her wits, Lucy muttered, 'I'm going to do the dishes first, they won't take long.'

He stood up. 'I'll give you a hand.'

As he stretched lazily, a bare strip of skin showed itself between his waistband and his T-shirt. She dragged her gaze away. 'You don't have to do that.'

'Two confrontations with Raymond Blogden today, along with a yelling match with me, is more than enough for one woman. Come on, let's get at them.'

'You can be so darn nice when you forget about being angry,' Lucy blurted, then, before he could reply, ran on, 'I know—I shouldn't have said that. My sisters always tell me I speak before I think, and they're right. They're right about nearly everything,' she added gloomily, 'it's very depressing. But it seems such a waste when you could be nice all the time.'

'You'd be bored,' Troy said. Then he raised one brow in mockery as he gathered the dessert dishes from the table. 'Besides, I was just practising for when our guests arrive.'

And that, thought Lucy, was that. After picking up the leftover chocolate sauce, which now looked sickeningly sweet, she followed Troy down the stairs.

CHAPTER THREE

LUCY woke at daylight. She knew exactly where she was as soon as her eyes opened. On board *Seawind* in Road Harbor. With four weeks ahead of her to cruise the Virgin Islands.

She jumped out of bed, filled with the tingling anticipation she had felt as a little girl every Christmas Eve. Except that this time she was the one who'd given herself a gift. The gift of time, she thought fancifully. What better gift was there?

Although even Christmas Eve hadn't always been trustworthy, she remembered, her hands faltering as she pulled on her darkest shorts. Her father had died when she was three, and confidently, at three, four and five, Lucy had requested Santa Claus to bring him back. Only when her elder sister Marcia had laughed at her efforts had she ceased to hope that she would find him early in the morning under the Christmas tree among all her other presents.

She gave her head a little shake. She rarely thought of her father now. And she had a lot to do today. Reaching up to look out of the open port, she saw that the sun was already glinting on the water, and again she was swept with excitement. When she went to the supermarket today she'd leave a message on her mother's answering machine, explaining her change of plans, then she was free. All she had to do was work hard and have fun.

And keep her temper with Tory Donovan.

She could handle Troy. She was through with big blond men.

Just as everything had gone wrong the day before, today the gods were with Lucy. Before she left for town, the galley, the brass and the woodwork were all gleaming with cleanliness. Near the delicatessen she found a spice shop that sold a series of recipe books with all sorts of suggestions for easy and tasty meals and aperitifs—just what she needed. She bought the first volume and several bottles of mixed spices, had a lemonade in a little restaurant and drew up her menus, then hit the deli and the supermarket.

It gave her great pleasure to stow everything away in her tidy galley. In the tiny microwave over the gas stove she heated *rotis* for lunch—West Indian sandwiches stuffed with curried chicken and vegetables, that tasted delicious washed down with ginger ale. Troy had been scrubbing the deck and polishing the winches; they ate in a silence that she was quite prepared to call companionable. When she'd cleared away the dishes, she tackled the three cabins that led off the saloon.

She was down on her knees wiping the floor of the aft cabin's shower when Troy spoke behind her. 'Let's take a break, Lucy.'

She glanced round, swiping at her hair with the back of her hand. 'How does it look?'

'You've done wonders,' he said.

His praise gave her a warm glow of pride. 'I've had a ball, actually—the woodwork and the fittings are all so beautiful that it's a pleasure to clean them. Much more fun than cleaning my apartment.' She sat back on her heels, stripping off her rubber gloves. 'What was that about a break?'

'I have to run the engine a couple of hours every day to keep the refrigerator and freezer cold. I thought we might head for Peter Island and have a swim. What have you got left to do?'

'The saloon floor. Make the beds and put out the towels.' Lucy tilted her head to one side. 'You did say swim, didn't you?'

She had managed to coax from him one of his reluctant smiles—a smile that, oddly, hurt something deep within her. He looked at her bucket and sponge. 'I hate to tear you away from something you're enjoying so much.'

'For you, I'll make the sacrifice.' She got to her feet. 'Will you show me how to snorkel?'

He looked surprised. 'You don't know how?'

'Troy, I've never been further south than Boston in my entire life. Everything down here's new to me.'

Her forehead was beaded with perspiration and there was a smudge of dirt on her chin, but her eyes were dancing and her smile was without artifice. Troy said slowly, 'You're making up for lost time, aren't you?'

She wouldn't have expected such discernment—or even interest—from him. Her heart beating a little faster, she said, 'I guess I am. These four weeks seem like time out. A break from my normal life. I—I seem to have lost my sense of direction somewhere along the way.'

As though the words were torn from him, he said, 'You're not alone there.' Then he raked his fingers through his hair. 'Let's pull up anchor and get out of here.'

No more revelations, Lucy realized, and knew better than to push. 'I'll dump the bucket and be right there,' she said. But for a moment she stood still, watching him stride across the saloon and up the steps. His leg muscles were those of a runner, but what was he running from? And how had he lost his way?

* * *

Once they were anchored off the beach at Peter Island, Lucy went below to put on her swimsuit. She had bought it—acting on another of her impulses—in the middle of a hailstorm in March. It was, in direct consequence, a bright red and quite minimal bikini. If she'd known about Troy Donovan, she thought, trying without success to cover even a fraction of her cleavage, she'd have purchased a staid one-piece. In an innocuous shade of beige. She pulled a white sport shirt over the bikini and went up on deck.

But the wind instantly whipped the shirt away from her body. As Troy turned around, about to say something, his jaw dropped, and he gaped at her as though someone had hit him hard in the chest. She was tall and full-breasted, her hips ripely curved, her long legs tapering to narrow ankles and feet. As an adolescent Lucy had hated her body, for she had shot up at the age of thirteen, towering over the boys in her class yet having to endure their covert and not-so-covert sniggers at her generous breasts. She had wanted to be tiny and delicate and feminine, like Tanya Holliday.

In the intervening years she had more or less made peace with her build. But right now she felt absurdly self-conscious, as though she were fourteen again. Grabbing at the shirt, she yanked it over what felt like an immense expanse of bare flesh.

This gave her something to do. Because if Troy was staring at her, she was struggling hard not to return the compliment. Under his taut belly his dark green trunks sat low on his hips; any attempt to regard his torso as nothing but neatly delineated groups of muscles—like the diagrams in her anatomy text—was a miserable failure. She said weakly, 'Where's the snorkeling gear?'

He snapped his mouth shut, knelt down and began hauling fins and masks out of a storage hatch. The wind played with his thick, unruly hair. Lucy quickly found a pair of fins that fit, then Troy passed her a mask. 'Try this one. Keep your hair out of the way—when you breathe in through your nose, the mask should stay airtight.'

The first mask was too big. As she pulled on the second Troy came closer, checking the seal. 'That looks good,' he said. 'You put this piece in your mouth and clamp your teeth over it. If water gets in the tube, throw your head back and breathe out hard.'

He was standing so close to her that Lucy was having difficulty breathing at all. Fighting to subdue her pleasure in the way Troy towered over her, she nodded her understanding of his instructions.

'The reef's to our left,' he added. 'I'm going to dive down and check that the anchor's holding, then we'll head over there.'

He pulled on his own fins and slid off the transom of the boat into the water. Lucy shed her shirt and followed with rather less grace; with her fins flapping in front of her and an undignified splash she fell forward into the sea. But she soon discovered that the fins added immeasurably to her speed, and by the time Troy surfaced with a thumbs-up sign she was over the reef. She dunked her mask into the water and gave a gasp of delight.

Below her in the clear turquoise water big purple sea-fans waved in the current, and a coral that looked like nothing so much as ostrich feathers swayed lazily back and forth. Patterns of sunlight danced on the white sand. Through the prongs of a hard coral shaped like antlers a school of fish darted; when they turned as one, their scales flashed with the iridescence of sapphires. Lucy opened her mouth to tell Troy about them, swallowed seawater as bitter as Epsom salts and raised her face, choking.

Immediately, it seemed, Troy was beside her. 'You okay?'

She spat out the water and the mouthpiece. 'The fish—they're like jewels!'

His own mouthpiece was hanging by his ear and he had pushed his mask up. 'Indeed. But when you're underwater you'd better keep your mouth shut—unless you want an early supper.'

'Yuk,' she said. 'I never did like sushi.'

'And, seriously, don't brush against any of the corals. Fire coral can sting you quite badly.'

'I won't.' Flashing him another smile before she adjusted her equipment, she struck out again. There were fish everywhere: black, yellow, silver, red and blue, small and large, striped, spotted and lined. Fascinated, she hovered over the shelves and crenellations of the corals, then Troy gestured to her and she swam over to him, forgetting how little of her body the bikini covered, ignorant of how gracefully she moved, her limbs all pale curves, her cleavage shadowed. Following his pointed finger she saw three small pink squid fluting through the water, their huge eyes, like silver coins, riveting her gaze.

Impetuously she surfaced again, shoving her mask away from her face. 'Thank you *so* much for bringing me here, Troy!' she sputtered. 'It's unimaginably beautiful—like another world.' But then her voice died away. 'What's the matter?'

He said with a savagery that frightened her, 'You're the one who's unimaginably beautiful.' The flat of his hand hard against her back, he pulled her closer, the water swirling between them. Then he bent his head and kissed her wet lips, his mask bumping against hers, his arm heavy across her shoulders.

Her fear vanished. It was as though all the wonders she had just seen, all the brilliant hues of the fish and of the corals, had exploded in her body in a wild kaleidoscope of color, and for a split second that was outside of time Lucy was consumed by an all-powerful and all-consuming happiness. But, as suddenly as he had seized her, Troy thrust her away, his heavy breathing overriding the splash and ripple of the sea. He looked as though he hated her, she thought blankly, and could not, for the life of her, think of a word to say.

'We'd better go back,' he grated. 'We've still got a lot to do.' As if he was being pursued by sharks, he began stroking toward *Seawind* in a strong overarm crawl.

Lucy, barely remembering to tread water, stayed where she was. She was about as adept a judge of character as she was a gourmet cook, she decided. Never, in a thousand years, would she have anticipated that kiss.

Troy hated her. So why had he kissed her?

Or did he hate her because he'd kissed her?

She had no answers to either question, and she could see him hauling himself up on *Seawind's* stern. She didn't think he'd leave her behind. But then what did she really know about the man called Troy Donovan?

Painfully, pitifully little.

Once she'd washed the salt water from her body with the transom hose, Lucy winched in the anchor and disappeared below to get changed. She was pegging her wet swimsuit to the lifeline that ran round the hull when Troy finally spoke to her. 'You can call that kiss temporary insanity or insatiable lust or just plain curiosity...I really don't care. I assure you it won't happen again.'

There was as little feeling in his voice as if he were discussing the lunch menu. Carefully not looking at him, because if she did she wasn't sure she'd be answerable for the consequences, Lucy went below decks and started washing and buffing the mahogany floor of the saloon. When they reached the harbor, she went to the forepeak and used the agreed hand signals to anchor *Seawind*. No need for conversation there. Afterward, she finished the floor, made two of the three beds with fresh sheets and threw together a shrimp salad for supper—activities that kept her busy and out of Troy's way, but did nothing to tame the tumult of emotion in her breast.

She was bent over the refrigerator, wondering where she'd hidden the bottles of dressing, when a sixth sense told her Troy had come downstairs and was watching her. Feeling her scalp crawl, not looking at him, she said, 'Ten minutes and we can eat.' As she moved two blocks of cheese to one side she saw the yellow caps on the dressing and pulled the bottles out. 'Good, there they are.'

'What the devil happened to your arms?' he demanded.

She put the bottles on the counter and clicked the hatch shut. 'What are you talking about?' she said, glowering at him.

He stepped on to the narrow strip of floor between the stove and the sinks, crowding her into the corner. 'Those bruises—how did you get them?'

Craning her neck, Lucy for the first time saw the ugly purple blotches high on the backs of her arms. Involuntarily she shivered, knowing exactly how she'd gotten them. 'Blogden—when he grabbed me, his rings dug in.'

Troy's epithet was unprintable. But Lucy wasn't in the mood to be impressed. 'I wonder what *his* motive was,' she said shrewishly. 'Temporary insanity, plain curiosity or insatiable lust?'

There was a small, deadly silence. 'Are you comparing me to him?'

As clearly as if it had just happened Lucy remembered how Troy's kiss had filled her with a joy as many-hued and vivid as the fish, and how everything he had done since then had repudiated that joy. She was honest enough to know she was as angry with herself as with him—for she'd been the one to feel the joy, she who had sworn off tall, blond men. She didn't want to fall in love again, it hurt too much and got her nowhere. She said, 'I am, yes. Although overall I'd have to say he showed more emotion than you.'

'Don't push me, Lucy.'

'Why did you kiss me, Troy?'

'I gave you three good reasons.'

'I want the real one.'

'I already gave it to you,' he said with a wolfish smile. 'Insatiable lust.'

Her knees were trembling. Bracing them against the cupboard door, Lucy said, 'You're the one who said no male-female stuff between us.'

'Haven't you ever wanted something—or in this case, someone—so badly your whole body told you what it wanted?' he quoted mockingly.

Lucy paled. 'You know what's so horrible about all this?' she demanded, with sudden, searing honesty. 'I liked you kissing me. I wanted you never to stop.' She dashed at the tears that had filled her eyes. 'What a stupid idiot I am ... because you're nothing but a cold-blooded manipulator. You wouldn't recognize an emotion if you fell over it.'

If her vision hadn't been obscured by tears she might have seen Troy flinch. But all he said was, 'So you're not quite as immune as you thought you were. Maybe we should sleep together, Lucy—then you could add me to your total. One more blond hunk to notch in your belt. Or wherever it is you keep tally.'

There was plenty of emotion in his voice now, and all of it was anger. 'No, thank you,' she said, as steadily as she could. 'I'm a little more discriminating than that.'

'That wasn't the impression I got.'

That he should so misread her hurt horribly. She wasn't one bit immune, she thought wretchedly, and knew she had to end this. Turning, she cut three slices of bread with a reckless disregard for safety, plastered them with butter, put two on Troy's plate and one on hers, then put the butter back in the refrigerator. How could she possibly have woken this morning feeling as if it was Christmas Day? More to the point, how on earth was she going to get through the next four weeks?

'I'm going to eat in my cabin,' she said, picking up her plate of salad and a glass of water. 'Kindly get out of the way— I already told you the galley was my turf.'

But Troy stayed where he was, blocking the narrow little passageway with his body. 'You said you liked me kissing you. But that wasn't because it was *me*. It was because I'm big and blond and male. Admit it, Lucy— you've stereotyped me from the first minute you saw me.'

With a cold clutch at her heart Lucy knew his words had touched a nerve. Were they true? Was he just one more in the succession of blond men she had fallen in love with? Fruitlessly. Quite often unrequitedly. And most certainly, except for Phil, chastely.

But compulsively. That was the awful part about it. She didn't seem to have any choice.

Taking her courage in her hands, she met his eyes. 'I don't want that to be true,' she said in a low voice. 'I'm trying to break that pattern.'

'I'd say you're a long way from succeeding,' he rasped.

A sudden wave of exhaustion swept over her, the same exhaustion that had so debilitated her while she'd had the flu. She stared hard at the front of his shirt. 'I'm tired, Troy. Please move so I can sit down and eat.'

'The only time you call it quits is when you don't want to face the truth—right, Lucy?'

She bit her lip, and said with sudden fierceness, 'Don't push your luck! I can leave *Seawind* you know. Anytime. And then who'll you get to cook for you?'

'You can't leave,' he said levelly, 'anymore than I can fire you. We're committed to the next four weeks on *Seawind*—and to each other. And don't ask me what I mean by that because I don't have a clue.' He backed up so that she could leave the galley and added testily, 'You'd better go to bed early tonight. It's not much of an advertisement for a cruise boat if the cook looks like she's on the verge of collapse.'

He wasn't worried about her, Lucy thought bitterly, crossing to her cabin and ostentatiously closing the door behind her. He was only worried about what his customers would think.

At least she and Troy wouldn't be able to fight while the Merritts were on board.

Lucy wasn't sure what she'd expected of her first set of guests. Two city sophisticates in designer cruise wear? Frazzled by high-powered careers and bored by anything less than the spectacular?

The reality couldn't have been more different. Heather Merritt was in her early thirties, a pretty and slightly overweight blonde who was openly delighted with *Seawind*; her husband Craig, also a little heavier than was healthy and perhaps ten years older than his wife, was a very ordinary-looking man until he smiled at his wife—his face then was so suffused with love that Lucy was moved.

She and Troy took them down to the saloon, offering them their choice of the three cabins. 'How beautiful everything is!' Heather exclaimed, taking in the basket of fruit that Lucy had arranged that morning, the neat shelf of paperbacks over the couch and the shiny mahogany fittings that were polished to perfection. 'Isn't it lovely, Craig?'

'Fantastic,' he said, squeezing his wife's hip.

She blushed. 'We'll take one of the two front cabins. Is that all right, darling?'

'Perfect.'

'The aft cabin has a slightly bigger bed,' Lucy said.

Heather's blush deepened. 'Oh, we like to cuddle up,' she said artlessly. 'We're on our honeymoon.'

'Married a week ago,' Craig said fondly, nuzzling his wife's neck. 'Let's take the cabin on the right, honey. You were standing to the right of that table in the library the very first time I saw you.'

Heather wound her arms around her husband's neck. 'I didn't know you remembered that!'

'I've never forgotten anything about you,' he declaimed, and kissed her with more ardor than was perhaps appropriate.

Troy muttered, 'I'll be on deck, Lucy, if you need me,' and made his escape.

When Heather had unwound herself from the embrace, Lucy ushered them both into the cabin, showing them the towels and the storage space and demonstrating how to pump the head and the shower. 'If you want to use both forward bathrooms, you're welcome to... and you might want to keep your bags in the other cabin, too. I think Troy plans to go to Peter Island for lunch, so you could come up on deck anytime you're ready.'

The Merritts did come up on deck, twenty minutes later. Heather's cheeks were rosy and Craig looked very pleased with himself; Lucy was quite sure they hadn't just been unpacking their bags.

Her main job at this juncture, Troy had informed her that morning, was to set their guests at ease; he wasn't planning to hoist the sails until after lunch, so she had nothing else to do. Since part of Lucy's success at massage was her genuine warmth toward people, she enjoyed chatting with the Merritts, pointing out various features of the boat as she did so.

'The agenda's totally up to you,' Troy intervened. 'Night-life, dining at resorts, beaches, swimming, hiking... Whatever you'd like to do most.'

'I want to dance to a steel drum band,' Heather said promptly.

'We can do that on Virgin Gorda—probably tomorrow night.'

'Snorkel,' Craig added.

'Right after lunch. I'll make sure you have the chance to swim with sea turtles, too.'

'I think we'd rather eat on board than go to fancy resorts, wouldn't we, darling?' Heather said.

'Whatever you want, babe,' her husband said, toying with the nape of her neck.

'Have you snorkeled before?' Troy asked smoothly.

'I have,' Craig replied. 'You haven't, have you, Heather?'

'You can teach me,' Heather said.

They exchanged a look so charged with sexuality that Lucy found she was the one who was blushing. She had worried about having to awaken the jaded appetites of a pair of New Yorkers; she hadn't anticipated that their appetites, so obviously carnal, might be more than she could handle. Glad of the cool wind on her cheeks, she remarked, 'Did you meet in New York?'

For the next ten minutes the Marritts regaled them with the story of their romance, from their meeting in a branch library in Manhattan to the first part of their honeymoon in a hotel at the west end of Tortola. 'A pool surrounded by palm trees,' Heather said ecstatically. 'It was wonderful... New York had more snow this winter than the last five years.'

'Remember the snowstorm that marooned us in your apartment for two days?' Craig murmured.

Heather giggled, Craig rested her fingers on his thigh and started playing with them, and Troy kept his gaze on the hills of Peter Island. He anchored in the same spot where he and Lucy had snorkeled yesterday. Where he had kissed her, Lucy thought, suddenly not able to bear watching the Merritts for a moment longer. 'Lunch in ten minutes,' she said briskly, and vanished below.

They ate on deck. Lucy served *rotis* with salad, chutney and hot sauce from the spice shop, following this with sliced mango and melon decorated with strawberries. The Merritts relished everything, and insensibly she relaxed. While she cleaned up the dishes in the galley, Troy fitted their guests with snorkeling gear. 'Are you going swimming, Lucy?' he called down to her.

'No, I'm going to make dessert for tonight.'

'Okay, I'll leave you in charge.'

A few minutes later, after the Merritts had changed, she heard the dinghy chugging away from the stern. She had *Seawind* to herself, she thought, feeling the tension that Troy seemed to cause by his very presence slowly seep from her body. She mixed a crumb crust, pressed it in a pie plate and put it in the oven, then soaked gelatin and began cracking ice to make the filling for a rum chiffon pie—tasks that soothed her further. Because, back home in Ottawa, she had chosen not to share her apartment, she was used to spending time every day by herself. It was nice to be alone now. Humming to herself, she separated four eggs and beat the whites into frothy peaks.

Had Troy been right when he'd accused her of not seeing him for himself? Her hands stilled. Had he—and this hadn't occurred to her before—been hurt that she'd bracketed him with the other men who'd passed through her life? Just another blond hunk? One more to add to the list?

Not hurt. Not Troy.

She added sugar and a generous measure of West Indian rum to the egg whites. The crust was cooked, so she put it to cool, and while she was waiting mixed cream cheese with sour cream and mayonnaise as the base of the crab dip she planned to serve with drinks before dinner. As long as she could stay organized she wouldn't get in a panic, as she had the night of the curdled hollandaise.

What had Troy meant when he'd said they were committed to each other? *Could* she quit?

She wasn't sure she could. And what did that mean?

CHAPTER FOUR

THE next twenty-four hours tested Lucy's fortitude to the limit. While she liked the Merritts, both individually and as a couple, she could cheerfully have wished their sex-lives to the bottom of Sir Francis Drake Channel. They were never more than three feet away from each other, they were frequently entwined, and she was quite sure that if she and Troy hadn't been there they'd have made love in the galley, the cockpit and the dinghy.

The saloon was by no means soundproof. She had gone to bed to the sound of enthusiastic coupling and had woken in the night to hear Heather moaning her husband's name in what was clearly a state of ecstasy. The only one of the blond hunks with whom Lucy had gone to bed had been Phil, when she had been engaged to him; it had been, in general, a pleasant enough experience, but she couldn't for the life of her recall making, or even wanting to make, sounds so redolent of unbridled passion.

If she were to make love with Troy, though... And here Lucy's thoughts had slammed to a stop.

The worst part about having the Merritts aboard was the way it made Lucy achingly and constantly aware of Troy: the breadth of his shoulders in the tank top he had worn all day, the neat set of his ears, the shining cleanliness of his hair, blown dry by the wind, even the way his high-arched feet clung to the companionway steps. His feet, for goodness' sake! When had she ever noticed a man's feet before? When had the sight of a man's pulse beating in the hollow of his wrist made her weak with longing?

Never.

The trouble was, she was almost sure Troy reciprocated every one of her feelings. He'd brushed against her last night when she was serving dinner, and had backed off as if he'd put his hand on the blue flames of the gas stove rather than on her elbow. When they had all been swimming, late yesterday afternoon, she'd caught him staring at the swell of her breasts in her red bikini as though he'd never seen a woman before.

Tonight all four of them were supposed to go dancing. Craig and Heather would no doubt spend the evening wrapped in each other's arms on the dance-floor. What would she and Troy do?

She mixed a rum punch decorated with cherries and pineapple for Craig and a pina colada for Heather and put them on a tray, along with the crab dip and crackers. Up on the deck Craig had his arm around Heather, whose head was resting on his shoulder. Troy had his back to them, lighting the barbecue that was attached to the stern rail; he was going to grill fillet steaks for dinner. 'Beer, Troy?' Lucy asked.

'Sure... thanks.'

She climbed to the cooler near the hatch of his cabin and took out a can of beer, and when she got back to the cockpit, opened it. Heather was feeding Craig a cracker laden with dip, her tongue licking her lips, her gaze locked with his. Lucy's eyes skidded away and met Troy's. As she passed him the can of beer their hands touched, and she felt a jolt of naked desire lance along her nerve-endings. She snatched her hand back and saw the same raw need flare in the slate gray of his irises, lustrous as sunlight falling on the smooth surface of a rock.

She fled back to the galley, to the ordinary demands of baking potatoes and wrapping up onions brushed with curry powder to go on the barbecue. She could hear music playing in one of the boats moored near *Seawind*... Would Troy dance with her tonight at the yacht club? Maybe he was no more prepared to risk that than she was.

She was mixing the salad dressing when Troy came down to get the barbecue sauce. He crouched down to rummage through the cupboard; she could have run her fingers through his hair. She said brightly, 'How long before you're ready?'

'Fifteen minutes.' He gave a grunt of satisfaction and stood up. 'You've got flour on your face,' he added, reaching out one finger to wipe her cheekbone.

Unconsciously Lucy swayed toward him. Very deliberately he put the bottle of sauce on the counter, rested his palms on her shoulders and drew her closer. She knew he was going to kiss her; with the softness of her lips, the pliancy of her body, she welcomed him. And then she was drowning in a host of sensations new to her: his height, the burning heat of his mouth moving against hers, the strong clasp of his fingers and the frantic beating of her own heart.

'Oh...sorry,' said Heather. 'I didn't mean to interrupt.'

Lucy froze, Troy wrenched his mouth free and Heather gave a coy giggle. 'You two are so discreet,' she said admiringly. 'We didn't even realize you were a number.'

'We're not!' Lucy gasped.

'Discretion's my middle name,' Troy drawled.

'There's nothing to be discreet about,' Lucy flared.

'Didn't look that way to me,' Heather said.

'Nor me,' Troy murmured, and with a reckless gleam in his eye laid claim to Lucy's lips again.

She tried to push him away. But his chest was as hard as the teak in the cockpit, and as his tongue flicked against her teeth her traitorous hands crept up to busy themselves in his hair. She had, she thought dimly, been longing to do that for the last three days. From a long way away she heard the stairs creak; Heather, presumably, was leaving. Only then did Troy release her, taking his time about it, drinking in the feverish glitter in her eyes, the patches of pink staining her cheeks. He said, '*That* feels better,' picked up the barbecue sauce and followed Heather up the stairs.

Lucy sat down hard in the nearest swivel chair. She'd done it again, she thought, horrified. She'd fallen under the spell of a big, blond man. How *could* she have?

The scent of grilled meat drifted to her nostrils. After kissing her until she'd thought she'd die with pleasure, Troy was now barbecueing as if nothing had happened. Not sure whether she wanted to laugh, cry, or stamp her bare feet on the polished floor, she somehow, in the next fifteen minutes, managed to mix the salad dressing and lay the table in the saloon with a pretty green cloth and an array of wine-glasses and cutlery. If only to keep thought at bay, she folded flowered napkins into shapes like little sailboats and hibiscus blooms.

Cute, Lucy. Really cute.

Rather to her surprise, all the food was ready at once and it all tasted delicious. Troy poured a more than respectable burgundy and kept the conversation flowing on such impersonal topics as the history, wildlife and music of the Virgin Islands. Afterward Lucy cleaned up the galley, banging the dishes around and splashing the water as much as she could to hide Heather's squeals as she and Craig got changed. Then she went to her own cabin and shut the door.

She could wear a pair of unexceptional beige linen trousers and a loose blouson top, or she could wear her favorite sundress, which did rather cling in all the right places and was a rousing shade of tangerine.

She was in the tropics. She was going dancing with the most attractive and disturbing man she'd ever met, a man who had kissed her and walked away from her without a backward look and hadn't once, during dinner, by word or gesture, remotely referred to that kiss. From experience Lucy knew she attracted attention when she wore that dress—at least Troy would know she was on the same planet.

Last, but by no means least, in three and a half weeks she'd be going back to all the predictabilities and responsibilities of her life in Ottawa.

No contest.

When Lucy went on deck twenty minutes later the others were waiting for her. While her sundress had a flared skirt that went to midcalf it was sleeveless and low-cut in both the front and the back; gold jewelry glittered at wrist and ear and makeup gave her eyes a mysterious depth and her cheeks a soft glow.

Craig emitted a shrill wolf whistle as Heather said unaffectedly, 'How beautiful you look, Lucy! Doesn't she look beautiful, Troy?'

'Very,' said Troy, without a trace of emotion. 'Shall we go?'

All Lucy's pleasure in her appearance evaporated. He thought she was overdressed. He hated orange. He didn't want to go dancing with her.

He probably wished he hadn't kissed her.

She was the last one to get in the dinghy, casting off as she did so. Night had fallen while they ate. The lights of the yacht club glimmered on the waves and the rhythms of the band drifted across the water, exotic and compelling. The moon, a thick, creamy yellow, hung low in the sky.

The wind of their passage flattened Troy's blue shirt against his chest; his tailored cotton trousers were taut over his thighs. Lucy looked away and bent her head to catch something Heather had said. Maybe, she thought hopefully, Craig would tear himself away from Heather long enough to dance with her. She loved to dance, and it sure didn't look as though Troy was going to ask her.

The dance-floor was sheltered by a green and white striped canopy and was surrounded by tables under the rustling sheaves of the palm trees; as the fronds swayed gracefully in the breeze the stars appeared and disappeared. The scent of frangipani hung in the air. Troy ordered drinks and Craig asked Heather to dance. Troy and Lucy then sat, in complete silence, through the next three numbers.

A romantic setting was no guarantee of romance, Lucy decided, watching Craig whirl Heather in a circle and very much aware of what an uncomfortable emotion envy could be. Troy seemed to have his eyes glued to a young girl with straight blonde hair who was gyrating at the far corner of the dance-floor with a burly redhead. He was gripping his glass so tightly his knuckles were white.

The band struck up a lively calypso number. Feeling like the wallflower she had been at the age of thirteen, when she'd been three inches taller than all the boys in her class, Lucy snapped, 'It's obvious you don't want to dance with me—so why don't you ask her to dance?'

Troy's head jerked round. 'Who? What are you talking about?'

'The blonde you've been staring at for the last ten minutes—ask her to dance, Troy.'

She couldn't complain that she didn't have his attention now; he was glaring at her with such concentrated fury that Lucy shrank back in her chair. 'No,' he said with icy calm. 'I don't want to dance with her. Or with you, Lucy. Got that?'

Refusing to back down, she said, 'So you can kiss me any time you feel like it, but I'm not good enough to be seen with you in public, is that it?'

'Don't be an——'

'Craig and Heather are coming back,' she interrupted, giving him a smile of patent falsity.

'Dance with me, Lucy?' Craig asked.

Heather circled Troy's wrist and pulled him to his feet. 'It's a great band and I bet you're a fabulous dancer.'

As Craig jived with her Lucy kept catching glimpses of Troy and Heather, for they were only a few feet away; Troy was indeed a fabulous dancer and was giving every appearance of enjoying himself. Hurt and rage mingling in her orange-clad bosom, Lucy noticed out of the corner of her eye that the blonde girl and her red-headed partner had left. When the dance ended, amid a smatter of applause, Heather pulled Troy over to Lucy and said firmly, 'Your turn to dance with Lucy, Troy... Craig and I never switch partners for more than one dance in a row, do we, darling?'

Short of outright rudeness, Troy had no choice but to dance with her now, Lucy thought, inwardly furious with Heather for her interference. The music started, a much slower song, with a dreamy repetitive rhythm that was so far from Lucy's present state of mind that she didn't know whether to laugh hysterically or run from the dance-floor. Troy solved her dilemma by taking her in his arms. Holding her an impersonal distance from his body, he began to dance.

She wasn't sure which was worse: sitting in silence with him at the table, or dancing with him when he was only doing it to please Heather. Lucy knew a lot about touch, because it was her business. She loved the feel of Troy's hands—the smooth warmth of his palm, the latent strength of his fingers—and hated how that very strength was being used to keep her away. He had said not a word since Heather had foisted her on him.

She said amicably, 'You don't like my dress, do you?'

Troy's eyes slashed to her face. 'Whatever gave you that impression?'

'And you sure were telling the truth when you said you didn't want to dance with me. I don't have any communicable diseases, Troy.'

'You like the truth? Then I'll tell you the truth!' The fingers of his right hand dug into her hip as he scowled down at her. 'I don't scare easy, Lucy Barnes. But I was scared witless to take you out on the dance-floor. In that dress. In which you look ravishingly, gloriously, irresistably beautiful.'

'You *like* it?' she squeaked.

'Of course I do!'

'Oh.' Gaping at him like an idiot, she said, 'You were scared that if we danced together I might rip the shirt from your body?'

'I was probably scared you wouldn't.'

She tripped over his foot, lost her balance and grabbed at his elbows for support. 'I hate sewing on buttons,' she said. 'That's the downside of shirt-ripping.'

His voice thickening, he answered, 'No buttons on that dress of yours—all I'd have to do is haul it over your head.'

Giving up any attempt at dancing, Lucy stood stockstill in the middle of the dance-floor. Fluttering her lashes, she said, 'We might even teach Craig and Heather a thing or two.'

Troy suddenly threw his head back and began to laugh, a deep belly laugh that made him sexier than Robert Redford could ever have been and gave Lucy an inkling of what he might look like if only he were happy... Because, of course, Troy wasn't happy, she thought slowly. Something was eating at him, robbing him of vitality. Destroying any possibility of the light-heartedness she was now seeing and that touched her to the core.

Before she could even formulate any questions, he said, 'We're attracting attention. Maybe for now we should stay fully clothed and attempt a two-step...okay?'

She would have stood on her head to keep that smile on his face. Which was not, Lucy thought in puzzlement, the way she had ever felt with Phil. Or Wayne, who'd taught her to dance last year and had done his best to inveigle himself into her bed in the process.

She stopped thinking altogether when Troy drew her closer. Their two bodies moved in perfect unison to the music, its languorous throbbing an intimate part of the warm, moonlit darkness. The beat began to quicken. Troy pulled her toward him then whirled her away, clasped her by the very tips of her fingers, then held her by the whipcord strength of his arms, hard against the wall of his chest. The beat was intoxicating now, fierce and imperative—ancient rhythms of the jungle that were far less gentle than moonlight and intimate in a totally new way. Lucy let her body move as it would, her hips swaying in outright invitation, her hair swirling around her face.

Finally the song ended. Troy spun her in one last circle, so that she ended up with her back to his chest, his arms wrapped around her waist with an unspoken possessiveness that filled her with excitement. Into her ear he muttered, 'Next time I say no male-female stuff, you have my full permission to call me a liar.'

She loved the clasp of his fingers against her belly, the warmth of his breath stirring her hair. More than loved them. Hungered after them with an intensity that shocked her. Phil had made love to her; Wayne had danced with her. But she had never felt in a man's arms this unsettling mixture of utter safety and searing danger. She chuckled, twisting her neck so she could look into Troy's face and widening her eyes. 'Call the skipper a liar? You might maroon me on the nearest island with a keg of rum.'

'I might join you,' he said roughly.

Abandoning herself to a happiness that shimmered in her heart like moonlight on water, Lucy closed her eyes, the better to savor the sweetness of Troy's embrace. She could have wished the band, Heather and Craig, and all the other dancers and onlookers a thousand miles away. She wanted to be alone with Troy. Just the two of them and this growing tension in the soft, seductive night...

But then Troy said, 'Hell, who's that waving at me? It's Jack—you remember Jack. He ate all your crab dip the first night you were on board. We'd better go and say hello. Those must be his guests with him; he said his next charter was fully booked.'

Before she was ready for it, Lucy was plunged into a flurry of introductions that she never did succeed in straightening out. One of the young men asked her to dance. Troy had already settled down between Jack and a rather attractive brunette whose name was either Darlene or Charlene, so Lucy accepted. Action was better than sitting there watching Troy be charming to someone else, and feeling as though she'd just had a limb amputated because he wasn't holding her in his arms anymore.

What was wrong with her? She'd never felt like this in her life.

The young man was a flashy dancer; she had to concentrate if she wasn't going to disgrace herself. She danced two numbers with him, one with the husband of Darlene or Charlene, and then lumbered around the floor with Jack, who suffered from the classic complaint of two left feet. Troy didn't ask her to dance again.

Two rounds of drinks were ordered and consumed. Lucy danced some more. Then Heather yawned widely and said with an endearing laugh, 'Past my bedtime.'

Craig kissed her ear amorously and Troy got up. There was a round of farewells, and in a few minutes the four of them were heading back to *Seawind* in the dinghy.

When they got on board Troy included Lucy in his smile, without singling her out, and said, 'Goodnight, all... See you in the morning.' Craig and Heather disappeared into the saloon and Lucy was left alone in the cockpit.

She felt at once desperately tired and wide awake; she also felt both angry and deeply hurt. How could Troy wrap his arms around her on the dance-floor as if she was his heart's desire and then say goodnight to her as if she was no more to him than Heather?

And what was this male-female stuff he kept talking about? Nothing more than sex?

A profound depression settled like a shroud over all her other emotions. Screwing up her face like a gargoyle at the moon, which was now sailing serenely in the heavens, Lucy went to bed.

When Lucy woke it was still dark. She had been dreaming, a confused dream where she was serving crab dip to Charlene—or Darlene—on board a bright orange dinghy to the strains of a steel band. It's rhythmic thump-thump echoed in her ears. And then she sat bolt upright, instantly awake. It wasn't the steel band she was hearing. It was Craig and Heather.

She switched on the little brass lamp over her bed. Three a.m. They were sex maniacs, she thought, enraged. Didn't they have any consideration for someone like herself, who didn't have a man and who, moreover, had to get up early tomorrow morning to bake pineapple muffins for their breakfast?

She turned off the light, buried her head under her pillow and squeezed her eyes tight shut. But the thudding continued, until, unable to bear it any longer, Lucy picked up her pillow and blanket, opened her cabin door and marched up the stairs, ducking to avoid the closed hatch.

The cockpit was cool, and the slapping of waves against the hull smothered any other sounds. She arranged three padded cushions along the bench and curled up on them with her blanket and pillow, composing herself for sleep.

She was lying in the deep shadow of the bimini. But the moonlight shone white on the hull, and she suddenly felt inexpressibly lonely. She was twenty-five years old. She was hundreds of miles from all her friends, she had a family who loved her without understanding her in the least, and she had a history of choosing the wrong men.

A high percentage of her friends were married with children. Why wasn't she? What was wrong with her?

She might be furious with Heather and Craig for disturbing her sleep, and she might deride them at times as a typical honeymoon couple, but she was quite astute enough to see that they truly loved each other and were very happy in each other's company. She would have liked to know what that felt like.

The wind sang softly in the shrouds. The boat rose and fell on the waves. The first tear crept down Lucy's cheek. She pulled the blanket over her face and read herself a stern lecture on the perils of self-pity.

Something hit her hard on the shoulder. Flung sideways on the bench, Lucy gave a screech of fear utterly unlike Heather's lovesick cries and tried to struggle free of the folds of the blanket. A dark shape thudded on to the deck beside her. For the second time that night she sat bolt upright, her blood pounding in her ears, with fear, this time, rather than rage.

Then the shape cursed in a reassuringly familiar voice and resolved itself into a large blond man clutching at the table for support. Troy.

Who else?

Lucy said shakily, 'What do you do for an encore?'

'I didn't see you—you scared me out of my wits.'

'Not half as bad as you scared me.'

He ran his fingers through his hair. He was wearing a pair of very brief shorts and nothing else. Lucy clutched the blanket to her chin and heard him ask, 'Do you make a habit of sleeping up on deck?'

She lowered her voice. 'Only insofar as those two make a habit of lovemaking half the night.'

He sat down on the bench beside her. 'I know the feeling... How many times is this in the last twenty-four hours?'

'Four?'

'I thought it was five.'

'We could fight over it,' Lucy suggested, realizing that her heart was still racing even though she was no longer afraid. Or, at least, no longer afraid of an unknown intruder.

Troy said forcefully, 'It's like living in a bordello.'

'What I need,' Lucy responded thoughtfully, 'is a swim in the Pacific Ocean. In April, that's cold.'

'A five-mile run.'

'Watch *Psycho* three times in a row.'

'Fifty bench presses at one hundred pounds each.'

Lucy chuckled. 'Or maybe just an undisturbed night's sleep.'

'Yeah...' His eyes narrowed and he leaned forward. 'Lucy, you've been crying. What's wrong?'

She pulled back, wiping her cheeks with the blanket. 'Nothing!'

'Come on, surely we've progressed beyond that?'

She bit back an acid retort. 'Have we, Troy?' Playing with the silk-lined hem of the blanket, she added in a rush, 'Progress implies starting somewhere and ending up somewhere else. In a better place. I don't have any idea if you and I are going anywhere. Or even if there's anything between us.'

'There's sexual attraction for sure,' he said, in a voice raw with feeling. 'At the moment I can't get beyond that.'

It wasn't exactly the answer she had hoped for. But he had been honest with her. 'Male-female stuff,' she said drily.

He nodded. Making no move to touch her, he said with a matter-of-factness that was totally convincing, 'Right now I'd like nothing better than to take you to bed.' He hesitated. 'Would you go with me, Lucy?'

Her heart gave its own answer by leaping in her chest, and somehow the moonlight and the silence that underlaid the soft playing of the sea precluded anything but the truth. In a small voice she said, 'I guess so. Even though a couple of days ago you more or less accused me of promiscuity.'

WELLS FARGO ATM Transaction Record

STATEMENT OF BALANCES FOR LINKED ACCOUNTS   PAGE 1

CUSTOMER NO.
XXXXXX32.05

DATE   TIME   ATM NO   LOCATION
06.10.10   07:11 PM   98152X   FORT WAYNE, IN

DEPOSIT ACCOUNTS   NUMBER   TOTAL BALANCE   AVAILABLE BALANCE
CHECKING   XXXXXXXXXXXX9459 $98.93 $98.93

THANK YOU FOR BANKING AT WELLS FARGO BANK

With you at more than 12,000 Wells Fargo and Wachovia ATMs nationwide

Thank you for using a Wells Fargo ATM.

If you have any questions, please call
1-800-TO-WELLS (1-800-869-3557)
Business customers can call 1-800-225-5933

Visit **wellsfargo.com** to find a convenient
Wells Fargo store or ATM near you.

For non-account related ATM feedback,
email ATMs@wellsfargo.com

Printed on recyclable paper.   Group 1:04_10 VALPROP_210ww_0810

WELLS FARGO **ATM Transaction Record**

Date:	12/01/10
Time:	03:43 PM
Location:	FORT-WAYNE-LA
ATM:	5843Y

Customer Card:	xxxxxxx2205
Transaction #:	4488
Transaction Type:	Withdraw From Checking
Amount:	$40.00
From Account #:	xxxxxx3685
Available Balance:	$58.68
Total Balance:	$58.68

Thank you for using a Wells Fargo ATM.

Share your ATM comments or suggestions

Email us at:

@ ATMS@wellsfargo.com

For questions about your account, please call 1-800-TO-WELLS

Thank you for using a Wells Fargo ATM.

If you have any questions, please call
1-800-TO-WELLS (1-800-869-3557)
Business customers can call 1-800-225-5933

Visit **wellsfargo.com** to find a convenient
Wells Fargo store or ATM near you.

For non-account related ATM feedback,
email ATMs@wellsfargo.com

♻ Printed on recyclable paper.

ATMs_210ww_0810

'All these big blond men that you're so attracted to... didn't you sleep with them?'

'One of them. Phil. We were engaged at the time.'

'Only one? You're twenty-five, Lucy!'

'Only one.'

The breath hissed between his teeth. 'Why?'

She hugged her knees to her chest under the blanket. 'My mother had very strict standards. And I was always falling in and out of love, so I didn't really trust my own emotions... I suppose there's a certain poetic justice to the fact that Phil was the one to leave me. He ran off with one of those tiny, fragile little women who was everything I'm not.'

'I like you exactly as you are, and if you were any more beautiful I don't think I'd be able to stand it,' Troy announced.

'*What*?'

'You heard. Phil, in my humble opinion, was an idiot.'

'I think I've just received the very best compliment of my whole life,' Lucy said.

'I happen to mean it,' Troy replied in a clipped voice.

The very lack of feeling in his voice was what persuaded her; Troy, she was beginning to realize, combined honesty with locked-up emotion in a way that was disconcerting but very much part of him. Had she ever wanted to understand Phil as intensely as she now wanted to understand Troy?

She didn't think so.

She said, casually she hoped, 'Have you ever been married or engaged, Troy?'

'Engaged. Once. Never married.'

As the silence stretched out Lucy added in exasperation, 'Well, you can't stop there!'

'You're very curious, Lucy Barnes.'

'I'm interested, that's all,' she said loftily, trying to subdue what was undoubtedly jealousy at the thought of the unknown woman to whom Troy had been engaged.

'To understand the story of my broken engagement, you'd have to know my parents,' Troy said. His profile, with its strongly hewn nose and cleft chin, was turned to her; he was speaking as much to himself as to her. 'They've lived in Victoria all their lives. Good, law-abiding citizens, with—like your mother—very high standards. Strong emotion—emotion of any kind—they considered rather bad form. When I escaped to university in Toronto at the age of nineteen I sowed considerably more than the usual crop of wild oats. But eventually I got that particular rebellion out of my system and settled down, and then three or four years later Rosamund moved to Toronto. She was the daughter of my parents' best friends and my mother had never made any secret of her hope that Rosamund and I would marry. Rosamund was quiet and gentle and very lovely, and I was run off my feet at the time and in need of a little cherishing, so we started dating. One thing led to another and we got engaged.'

He turned to look at Lucy and said with sudden force, 'It wasn't enough! She wasn't enough. I knew that almost immediately. But I didn't want to hurt her, and I kept hoping that somehow things would change. That my feelings would get out of hand instead of everything being so goddamned placid and low-key.' He grimaced. 'You can probably guess the rest. I started to feel trapped, confined...through no fault of Rosamund's—I never blamed her. I finally broke our engagement. And even though I felt like a louse, I also knew I'd done the right thing. For both of us. I'm not sure my mother ever understood, though. She kept asking what was wrong with Rosamund—and of course nothing was.'

Lucy's hands were cold, even under the blanket. 'What's happened to you since then, Troy?' she asked. 'Because you've taken all your feelings—except anger—and buried them. All those feelings that you wanted to express with Rosamund and couldn't.'

His short laugh was devoid of humour. 'Don't get too curious, Lucy.'

Her lashes flickered. 'You give intimacy with one hand and take it away with the other.'

'That's all I can do right now! And, for Pete's sake, don't ask me why.' He stood up abruptly. 'You're cold, you'd better go back to bed.'

She stood up too, the blanket loose around her shoulders. Her nightgown was made of thin white cotton decorated with old-fashioned lace; it reached only to mid-thigh and more than hinted at the swell of her breasts. She could have covered herself. Instead she waited, seeing the tension gather in Troy's mouth, the torment shadow his eyes.

Like a man who couldn't help himself he took two steps toward her and pulled her into his arms. The blanket slithered to the deck. Lucy circled his neck with her arms and lifted her face for a kiss whose pent up need did away with any vestige of resistance she might have felt. His lips burned into hers with all the heat of the noonday sun; her body melted and with every nerve she possessed she was aware of his hands roaming her ribcage, her waist, her hips. It was as if he couldn't bear for there to be space between them, as if body pressed to body and muscle strained against muscle was what the moonlit night and his own desperation called for.

She opened to the searching of his tongue and felt his hand seek the warm weight of her breast. Shifting slightly in his arms, she gave him what he wanted, and was re-warded, as he stroked the curve of her flesh, by a pleasure so strong as to border on pain. His erection pressed into her groin; her body ached with an emptiness that was more than just physical, and that only he could fill.

He was kissing her cheekbones, her hair, the slim length of her throat, passionate kisses, between which he was whispering her name like a mantra. And then with frantic haste he found her mouth again, imprinting himself on her so that she could know him as the shore knew the waves.

Like a streak of fire she felt his hand slide under her gown, traveling the tautness of buttock, the concavity of spine. Drowning in desire, she moaned his name, her hips of their own accord pressing into his with all her strength, moving back and forth in primitive and in-stinctual invitation.

The shock ran through his body. His hands grew still. Against her lips he muttered with anguished certainty, 'This is madness, Lucy—we can't do this!'

He cupped her shoulders, pushing her away. Her face was a battleground between bewilderment and desire, while her mouth was soft and swollen from his kisses. 'But I—I want you,' she stammered foolishly.

A pulse was hammering at the base of his throat. 'I want you, too—we both know that.' He took a step away from her. 'Come on, Lucy... You've only slept with one man before, and I outgrew going from bed to bed when I was twenty-one. Neither of us is into casual af-fairs and neither of us is in love with the other. Time to call it quits, wouldn't you say?'

'You sound so damned logical!'

'Why were you crying a while ago?'

She stooped and picked up her blanket, wrapping it around herself, all her movements short and jerky. 'I was lonely.'

'All the more reason for us not to make love,' he said grimly.

'For you, maybe. Don't speak for me.'

His voice rose. 'By God, you're argumentative.'

The pain of unfulfilled desire had all too swiftly translated itself into fury. Lucy retorted, 'Let me tell you something—I've never noticed you being either placid or low-key around me. Why don't you go to bed—by yourself, of course—and think about that, Troy?'

'Are you trying to tell me I'm in love with you?' he snarled. 'Don't be ridiculous! We've only known each other for four days and all we do is fight.'

Lucy swallowed hard. What she was really afraid of was that she was the one falling in love with Troy. A man she'd only just met, with whom she did indeed spend a lot of time arguing. The rest of the time she spent wishing he was in bed with her, she thought in horror, and prayed that he couldn't read her mind. Gathering her dignity around her, as if it were a blanket, she said with frigid politeness, 'Good night, Troy. I'll see you in the morning.'

'Okay, so you're different from Rosamund—so what?' he said harshly. 'And don't speak to me as if I'm something you found floating in the bilge.'

Lucy had often needed her sense of humor when dealing with a mother and two sisters who regarded her as a changeling. She said flippantly, 'Pardon me, Captain Donovan, sir,' and dropped Troy the best curtsy she could, swathed as she was in the blanket.

The glint in his eye had nothing to do with the moonlight. 'Goodnight, Lucy,' he said. Lightning-swift, he closed the distance between them and brushed his mouth back and forth with tantalizing slowness across her parted lips. 'Pleasant dreams,' he added, letting both hands trace the outline of her breasts under the blanket, watching her face change as he did so. Then lithely he climbed up on the bench and over the nearest hatch. Two seconds later he disappeared into his cabin.

Lucy, now that he was gone, thought of several very clever remarks she could have made. Her breasts were tingling, and as she ran a finger along the lips he had kissed so thoroughly she caught the faintest trace of the scent of his skin.

Heaving a huge sigh, she trailed toward the companionway steps. She felt frustrated, infuriated, upset and off-balance.

What she didn't feel was lonely.

CHAPTER FIVE

SOMEONE was knocking on Lucy's door, and the voice that had played havoc in her dreams was saying, 'Lucy—time to get up.'

Still half-asleep, Lucy leaped out of bed and yanked the door open. 'What's the matter?'

'Nothing.' Troy looked revoltingly wide awake, surveying her sleep-tousled hair and rumpled bed with a mockery that did nothing for her disposition. 'It's eight o'clock,' he said. 'Heather and Craig have taken the dinghy to go snorkeling in the cove—they'll be hungry when they get back.'

'Eight?' she repeated, horrified. 'It can't be!'

He said, an edge to his voice, 'Did you have pleasant dreams last night?'

It wasn't the moment to remember, with embarrassing clarity, the particularly compromising position she had found herself in with Troy in a dream that was a typical example of wish fulfillment. Lucy blushed scarlet and muttered, 'Go away!'

'So, you're argumentative first thing in the morning as well.'

'Troy,' she seethed, 'I have to make a fruit salad and muffins for our guests. Who also had an active night. Why don't you plug the coffee in? That would be far more helpful than standing there making personal remarks.'

'The coffee's already made,' he said tersely, took her by the shoulders and kissed her on the mouth.

73

He had used mint toothpaste and a herbal aftershave, and desire leaped rampant upon Lucy, like a tiger that had been lying in wait for its prey. As he pulled free of her she said faintly, 'If you keep that up, you'll be making the muffins—because I'll be taking a long, cold shower.'

'It's going to take more than a shower to get rid of what's between you and me,' he said, with a grimness that she deplored. 'Craig and Heather only just left the boat; you've got lots of time.'

Lucy said darkly, 'They're probably making love under the keel.'

Troy didn't smile; in fact, she wasn't sure he'd even heard her. 'Look,' he said, 'about last night. I think we should treat it as an accident, an aberration. Moonlight on water, altogether too much bare flesh, and our two busy little honeymooners raising our hormone levels to a peak. We should cool it, that's what I'm trying to say. Not get in that situation again.'

'Which is why you kissed me a moment ago,' she flashed.

'I kissed you because my thought processes go out the window when I'm within ten feet of you!'

'Good,' she said.

'Lucy, I'm serious.'

'I hate that word "should",' she said vigorously. 'I'm beginning to realize I've lived most of my life according to other people's "shoulds", and I'm sick and tried of it.'

'We are not going to have an affair!'

'I don't see why you have to fight me every inch of the way,' she cried. 'What is it that's got you so uptight? Why are you angry all the time?'

'Go to hell,' he said, and shut the cabin door in her face.

Lucy stamped her bare foot on the floor, winced from a pain that was entirely self-inflicted, and went into the bathroom to wash her face. Considering how many men she'd fallen in love with, a whole train of them ever since her grade seven history teacher, she knew nothing about men, she thought, glaring at herself in the tiny mirror.

Or, at least, nothing about Troy.

One thing was certain. She was behaving very differently with him than with any of the rest of them. So she wasn't in love with him. If that was any comfort.

It wasn't. She pulled on green shorts and a blouse which was wildly patterned in greens, pinks and yellows and that seemed to match her mood, and yanked her brush through her tangled curls. Big yellow earrings, a generous coating of pink lipstick, and she was ready for the fray.

Appropriate word, Lucy, she thought with a wry grin, and opened her door. To her great relief the saloon was empty. And to her great surprise the muffins, when she served them on deck an hour later, were excellent, as was the fruit salad she'd made to go with them. She sat as far from Troy as she could and made bright and bubbly conversation with Heather and Craig, and when the meal was finished she vanished belowstairs, feeling as though she'd already put in a hard day's work. Washing the dishes was soothing—the froth of suds and the hot water in the sink held no hidden messages, the neatly stacked and rinsed dishes were exactly as they appeared.

By the time she had cleared away breakfast, the Merritts had gone snorkeling again. Troy was sitting with his back to her at the chart table, bringing the log up to date. Wishing he'd gone snorkeling too, Lucy started rolling out a prepared package of puff pastry to make a strudel for dessert. Her hair fell forward in her face and she tucked it behind her ear, leaving a gob of dough stuck to it.

Troy said irritably, 'your hair shouldn't be so long when you're cooking all the time.'

He hadn't complained about it last night, when he'd had his fingers entangled in it and had been kissing her as if she were the only woman on earth. Stretching one corner of the pastry to make a right-angle, in no mood to be conciliatory, she snapped, 'More "shoulds". Is that your favorite word?'

'I'm the skipper; I'm allowed to use it. Get your hair cut when we're back in Road Town, will you?'

Abandoning the puff pastry, Lucy put her hands on her hips. 'And what if I don't want to?'

'The college crowd'll be arriving soon. Don't think of yourself as irreplaceable.'

His words cut through her anger, as perhaps he had intended. If he fired her she'd never see him again, she thought sickly, and was sure she hadn't felt so dead a weight of despair even when Phil had left town with Sarah. Hating the place to which her emotions had brought her, she hauled the cutlery drawer open, picked up the kitchen shears, which were as sharp as any of the knives in the galley, marched over to the chart table, seized a handful of the hair that hung over her left shoulder and cut it off.

Little wisps of hair drifted down on to the open pages of the logbook. Lucy was left with a clump of curls in her hand. Aghast, she said, 'I spent the last eight months growing this.'

Troy got to his feet. Standing very close to her, he said, 'You're like a volcano. One minute you're peacefully rolling out pastry, the next you're wielding a pair of scissors as if they're a machete.'

She tilted her chin. '*Would* you fire me?'

His voice was as sharp-edged as the scissors she was still clutching. 'Heaven help me, I don't think I can.'

'Well, that's a relief,' Lucy said. Gaping at the hank of hair, she added weakly, 'But that means I did this for nothing.'

'I'm not the easiest of bosses—I'd have thought you'd be delighted to be fired by me.'

'Then you'd have thought wrong.'

'Because I'm a big, blond man?'

'No.' She looked him straight in the eye. 'It's a lot more complicated than that, Troy—trust me. What am I going to do about my hair?'

'You infuriate me, you exasperate me, you're keeping me awake at night and on edge all day... and I can't damn well fire you,' Troy said. 'Will someone please explain that to me?'

A rueful smile curved her lips. 'Maybe we should ask our resident experts on male-female stuff—Craig and Heather.'

'I don't think that's a very good idea.' A fugitive smile lightened his features as he looked at the curls that were wrapped around her knuckles. 'You're going to have a hard time gluing those back on.'

'I'll have to try and cut the other side to match.'

'Sit down. I'll do it for you.'

His rare smiles always enchanted her. She glowered at him. 'Have you ever cut anyone's hair before?'

Troy hesitated, an odd look on his face that she was to remember later. 'Well, no, not exactly. But I'm sure I'll do a better job than you.'

'You could hardly do a worse one,' she answered gloomily. 'My mother had a quote, something to do with perverseness being a primitive impulse... Fits me to a T.'

'Why don't you get a comb and a towel from your room?' he said patiently. 'Unless you want to explain how you got such a lopsided hairdo to the honeymooners?'

She didn't. When she came back, Troy pushed her down in the chair and draped the towel over her shoulders. He worked quickly, with a deftness that fascinated her. 'Are you a hairdresser when you're not being a skipper?' she asked suspiciously.

'No. Hold still.'

His hands were warm on the back of her neck, and the small tugs of his fingers felt unbelievably sensual. Lucy closed her eyes, savoring each sensation. Troy said huskily, 'When the light strikes your hair, it gleams like bronze.'

'Your's is like gold,' she said.

'Yoohoo!' Heather called. 'Where are you?'

Lucy jumped and Troy cleared his throat. 'Down here,' he shouted.

Heather came tumbling down the stairs. 'Guess what— we saw three sea turtles. Lucy, you've got to—— Oh, your hair looks gorgeous! Troy, you're a marvel.'

Very carefully Troy removed the towel from Lucy's shoulders. 'Where were the turtles?' he asked.

'Way over on the far side of the cove... They were so beautiful, Craig took a whole roll of pictures. I love him dearly but he's not the best of photographers; I do hope we get one decent photo out of all that. Lucy, you must come and see them.'

Lucy scrambled to her feet. 'I've got to change my shirt and finish the strudel.'

'Darn the strudel! We can eat leftover muffins. This is more important, isn't it, Troy?' Shamelessly Heather batted her wet lashes at him.

Troy raised his brow. 'Off you both go—I know when I'm outnumbered.'

So fifteen minutes later Lucy was swimming over beds of wavering green grasses, where conch traced meandering paths along white sand that was dotted with spiny black sea urchins. Then a swifter, surer movement caught her eye. The turtle was stroking lazily over the grass toward the deeper water, its head and flippers speckled dark and light. The sun made flickering patterns of turquoise over its dull green shell.

She followed it at a safe distance, realizing how lucky she was to have entered a world not her own, and how privileged to be seeing an animal behave the way nature and instinct had ordained it to behave. Gradually the turquoise grew more opaque as the ocean floor fell away, until the turtle was lost to sight.

Filled with wonderment, she lifted her head. Heather wasn't ten feet from her. 'Lovely,' said Heather, and the two women smiled at each other. Heather added artlessly, 'That was kind of elemental, wasn't it? Like sex, in a way.'

'Oh?' Lucy said cautiously.

'Mmm ... I mean, I almost felt what it was like to be a turtle, swimming with one like that. As though I'd joined with it in some mysterious way. When Craig and I make love—which, when you think about it, is rather a peculiar act; whoever designed it must have had a sense of humour—this magical thing happens. We make love with our bodies but somehow our souls touch. We know each other, sort of like I knew the turtle.'

Any facetious comments Lucy might have made died on her lips. That was what had been wrong between her and Phil: their souls—whatever that word meant—had never touched. 'I see what you mean,' she mumbled, treading water and thinking what a peculiar place this was to be having a discussion about sex.

'You see, I don't think that kind of knowing happens very often. But I'm sure you and Troy could have it. I guess that's all I wanted to say—don't turn your back on something you might never find again.'

Heather was the customer; Lucy couldn't very well tell her to mind her own business. 'Troy and I aren't involved with each other!' she sputtered, as a wave slapped her in the chin.

'Piffle,' Heather said, pulling her mask back over her face. 'The vibes between you are as clear as—as this water... Oh, look, Craig's waving at us, shall we go back?'

Lucy took her time stroking toward the dinghy. Craig and Heather were in love, that would explain the kind of connection Heather had described. But she, Lucy, had loved Phil—hadn't she? So why had she experienced sex with Phil as a lack rather than a true joining? Whereas when she was with Troy, no matter what they did—argue, kiss or sail *Seawind*—she felt connected to him by a bond she could neither describe nor break.

She mustn't fall in love with Troy.

That would be one impulse she would bitterly regret.

For lunch the next day Troy steered *Seawind* to a beach on Copper's Island. Lucy arranged meats, cheeses and raw vegetables on a platter and served them with chutneys and wholegrain breads; she'd baked a banana loaf as well. After they'd eaten, Craig took the dinghy into shore. 'He wants to buy me something at the boutique,' Heather said fondly. 'He's such a sweetheart.' She took another sip of her orange juice and added, 'I've got a favor to ask you, Lucy.'

It was the Merritts' last full day, and if they'd made love the night before Lucy hadn't heard them. 'Fire away,' she said indolently.

'Troy told me you can do massage. Will you teach me how to massage Craig's back and shoulders? He spends so much time in front of his computer at work, I worry about him.'

'Sure, I'd be glad to. Whenever he comes back.'

'Well, I'd really rather surprise him.' Heather smiled with rather overdone innocence. 'You could demonstrate on Troy right now, couldn't you? You wouldn't mind, would you, Troy?'

Lucy dropped the celery stick she had been chewing. It was a set-up, she realized furiously, and could happily have pushed Heather overboard. 'I can't——' she began.

Troy almost knocked his can of Coke off the table. 'That's not such a——'

With another winning smile Heather overrode them both. 'Come on,' she coaxed, 'it won't hurt a bit.' She widened her eyes. 'And you'll get a fee massage out of it, Troy. If I were you, I'd be having Lucy give me one every day.'

Heather was one of nature's unstoppable forces, thought Lucy. Like the tides. Like the swell on the windward side of the islands. A man with a blond ponytail, whom she'd dated when she was nineteen, had had the same kind of unquenchable charm that seemed to brush aside the wishes of others as if they didn't exist. Knowing when she was beaten, she struggled to don her most professional manner and said, 'I've got some cream in my cabin. I won't be a minute.'

It was only skin cream, but it would do. When she went back up, Troy and Heather had moved forward to the padded green mats that were tied to the deck under the headsail, a place where those who still believed in tanning themselves could do so. Lucy spread her blanket over the mat and said with impersonal pleasantness, 'You'll have to take your shirt off, Troy. Then lie face-down, would you?'

Without once meeting her eyes, he did as she asked. Lucy put a pillow under his ankles and eased the waistband of his shorts part way down over his hips, quelling the incipient riot in her nervous system as she did so. She then said to Heather, 'I'll put the cream on first. When you're doing a massage like this, without a table, you must be careful of your posture.' Moving up to Troy's head, she took a couple of deep breaths, telling herself that Troy was no different from any other client.

Client? Who was she kidding?

She warmed the cream in her palms, making a huge effort to transpose herself back to her studio in Ottawa, away from the soft wind and turquoise sea that sur-rounded her. Swallowing, she said, 'The other thing to remember is how you make and break your contacts—no rough movements, no shocks. Like this.'

Leaning forward, she brought her palms down until they rested with exquisite gentleness on Troy's bare skin. She felt the shiver in his flesh and her own pulse leaped to meet it. Fighting down a response that all her training told her was utterly inappropriate, she smoothed the cream on with long strokes that ran from Troy's shoulders to the base of his spine. Her hands separated, circling the rise of his buttocks, then traveling along his ribcage and over his deltoid muscles back to the nape of his neck. His muscles had the tone of a man in the peak of physical fitness; the smoothness of his skin, his body heat, flooded her with wave upon wave of primitive hunger.

She said in her best teaching voice, 'You can see when I lean forward how my body weight comes into play—

I'm not just using my hands. You'll tire yourself out if you make all the strength come from your hands and wrists alone.' Leaving the fingertips of her left hand light on Troy's shoulder, she added, 'When I need more cream I keep contact with the client... You want him to relax, to trust you.'

Her words hung in the air, words meant more for Troy than for Heather.

Heather, to her credit, was paying close attention. Getting Lucy to massage Troy might have been a ploy; but her desire to learn was genuine enough.

Next Lucy kneaded the muscles in Troy's neck, one hand releasing its pressure as the other squeezed, working right up into his hairline where his blond hair, surprisingly soft, curled against his nape; she then smoothed the length of his spine again before deepening the pressure with long thumb-strokes all the way to his sacrum. 'Work on either side of the vertebrae,' she suggested, keeping to herself what she was learning about Troy's body as she worked on him. The tension in the deep layers of his musculature appalled her, and she could not flatter herself that it was sexual tension. Some of the more superficial tension might be. But most of it, she would have sworn, had been with him much longer than the week that he and she had known each other.

Anger, she thought. Anger and pain, caught and held for too long. Unwittingly—and no doubt unwillingly— Troy was revealing the secrets of his body to her.

When she moved to Troy's left side, to do thumb presses along his scapula, she felt him wince at the pressure she'd applied. 'Sorry,' she murmured, 'is this better?' He grunted, his eyes closed. Forgetting Heather, and forgetting for a few moments that this was Troy, Lucy brought her whole focus on to what she was doing, working with all her skill to release the tightness in his rhomboid muscles.

'It looks like that hurts,' Heather remarked.

'It's counterproductive to cause pain... But you don't want to be so gentle that you don't soften the muscles, either. After you've done deep work like this, it's a good idea to smooth it out.' Suiting action to words, Lucy glided her palm from Troy's neck over the long curve of his shoulder. Her hand wanted to linger; oh, God, when could she end this travesty?

'Now we'll increase the pressure along the spine,' she said evenly, resting her outer hand over her inner as she stroked to his tailbone again, letting her body weight do the work for her. It was a good thing it was broad daylight and they were out on deck, she thought with a tinge of real desperation. Not once in all the years she'd been giving massages had her own sexuality been an issue with any of her male clients. She'd rather prided herself on her professional detachment.

Not any more.

Knowing she was being precipitate, and unable to prevent herself, Lucy said, 'We'll finish up now—a few more long strokes, each one with less and less pressure. No abrupt moves, no sudden stopping.'

As she completed the last slow sweep of Troy's back, she rested one palm at the base of his neck, the other in the hollow by his pelvis. Then she gradually lifted her hands until the contact was broken.

Her whole body screamed its protest. She could have stayed there all day, she thought, and prayed that her emotions didn't show in her face.

'That was wonderful,' Heather exclaimed. 'Thanks, Lucy—and thank you for being the guinea pig, Troy. I'm going down to my cabin to write down everything you showed me before I forget.' Shading her eyes, she said, 'There's Craig, heading for the dock—I'll have to hurry.'

She scrambled to her feet, leaving Lucy and Troy alone. Feeling as self-conscious as if she'd just given her first massage, Lucy said, 'Want me to get another pillow for your head? Maybe you could sleep for a while?'

Troy pushed himself up on his elbows. The breeze ruffled his hair; his eyes were at their most opaque. 'I'm certainly in no state to get to my feet,' he said.

It was a split second before she realized that he had been as affected as she by their recent intimacy. Gathering her scattered wits, she mumbled, 'Just don't tell Heather, that's all I ask.'

His eyes narrowed. 'Did the two of you cook this up when you were snorkeling?'

'No! She cooked it up all on her own.' Carefully Lucy capped the bottle of cream. 'Heather thinks you and I belong together.'

'She couldn't be more wrong, could she?' Troy said with brutal emphasis.

Lucy said quietly, 'I don't know, Troy. I don't know much of anything when I'm around you.'

'That's at least one thing we have in common,' he jeered. 'Go away, will you, Lucy? I've got to get my act together. I'm supposed to be running this show. As soon as Craig gets back I want to head to Great Camanoe— we'll moor there overnight if the swell's not too high.'

He was the skipper and she was the crew, that was the message she was getting. Lucy pulled the pillow from under his legs and stalked toward the cockpit. She couldn't put her nose in the air; she might trip over one of the hatches.

At five to twelve the next day Craig brought the last piece of luggage up the stairs. *Seawind* was anchored at

the dock in Road Town. Heather asked Lucy to take a
photo of her and Craig holding the wheel, then said,
'Now I want one of you and Troy together.' She jumped
over to the dock, aiming the camera. 'Stand closer to
Lucy, Troy, and put your arm around her, or else I can't
get you both in... That's better.'

Lucy directed a strained smile at the lens. Troy's hip
was bumping hers and his grip had nothing of gentleness
in it. The minute the picture was snapped he let her go.
There was a flurry of hugs and promises to write, in the
middle of which Heather managed to whisper in Lucy's
ear, 'Be sure and invite me to the wedding.' Then,
waving, she and Craig walked away down the dock.

Lucy watched them go with mingled feelings. She
didn't need to be told how thoroughly they had enjoyed
Seawind and now they were happy to be by themselves
again. Would she, Lucy, ever be the most important
person in the world to a man whom she loved?

As she called one last goodbye she was aware of more
than a touch of regret. For all Heather's machinations,
Lucy had liked both her and her husband. Would she
ever see them again?

Certainly not at a wedding—the idea was laughable.

She turned back to *Seawind* and to Troy. Stepping into
the cockpit, she said, 'Now what?'

'At noon tomorrow the Dillons arrive. Victor and
Leona and their two teenagers, Kim and Brad. We've
got twenty-four hours to clean the boat from stem to
stern and reprovision her with food and drink for six
days.' Mockery twisted his mouth. 'Sure you don't want
me to fire you, Lucy?'

'I can handle it—but can you, Troy?' she responded
in deliberate challenge, and both of them knew she was
not referring to the Dillons.

'We'll have to share the forward cabin this trip,' he said, his eyes trained on her face.

She paled. 'What do you mean?'

'There are three cabins off the saloon. One for Victor and Leona, one for Kim, who's a girl, and one for Brad, who's a boy. None for you, Lucy. So you'll have to join me up front.'

She would have nowhere to hide from him. For five nights she would have to lie in her bunk listening to him breathing, tormented by his closeness yet unable to escape.

'You don't look very happy about it. Just be glad there are two bunks.'

She gave a cracked laugh. 'Wouldn't Heather just love this?'

Troy said softly, 'When you take the Jeep to town to get groceries, are you going to head for the airport instead?'

Lucy—and this was nothing new—had no idea what he was thinking. Maybe he wanted her on the first flight out of here? He'd made no secret of the fact that he hated the way she aroused him sexually, resenting her for having that much power over him. Her nerves lacerated, her throat tight, she suddenly felt all her energy drain from her body, as if she were a broken glass whose contents had spilled on the floor. She couldn't fight him anymore. She was tired of fighting him. And to what end? He always took more than he gave. And day by day she was getting more deeply embroiled.

Her shoulders slumped, she said, 'If you want me to go, Troy—really want me out of your life because you can't stand the sight of me—why don't you just say so? In the long run it would be easier. On me, for sure, and on you too, I suppose.'

'No,' he said.

She jammed her hands in the pockets of her shorts, her voice rising. 'No, what? No, it wouldn't be easier? Or no, you don't want me out of your life?'

He paused, as though he was searching for the precise words he wanted. 'Years ago I used to sail on the west coast, out of Victoria. The tides would pull the boat one way, the wind blow it another, and then a rain squall would hit and the wind would shift between one moment and the next... That's how you make me feel, Lucy.'

Her nails were digging into her palms. 'Nothing like the trade winds?' she ventured.

His smile was mirthless. 'Steady from the east at fifteen knots? No, nothing like that.'

Knowing the question held her fate, she asked, 'Did you give up sailing on the west coast? Because it was frustrating and full of risks?' And then stood still, waiting for him to answer.

Her legs were braced against the bench, her shoulders rigid. But her chin was raised and there was unconscious pride in the blue-gray depths of her eyes. Troy said flatly, 'I've only just realized what your eyes remind me of... They're the color of the sea in the Strait of Juan de Fuca, where I used to sail. No, I didn't give up sailing there. Even though it was dangerous and unpredictable, and every year a fisherman or a yachtsman would drown, I still went out.'

She let out her breath in a tiny sigh. 'That takes courage,' she said.

'My mother had a different word. She thought I was crazy.'

Feeling as though she'd been granted a reprieve at the very base of the gallows, Lucy laughed. 'At the risk of disagreeing with your mother, I'll stick with courage.'

He hesitated. 'It took courage for you to ask me if I really wanted you to leave, didn't it?'

She nodded. 'You might have said yes.'

'And that matters to you?'

'Oh, yes,' she said, astonished that he even had to ask. 'But I would have gone.' It was her turn to hesitate. 'When Phil was leaving with Sarah I begged him not to go, not to break our engagement. I guess what I learned then and what I've never forgotten is that it's useless to beg. I couldn't change Phil's mind—I couldn't change Phil. So I would have left Tortola, Troy. Left you. If you really hadn't wanted me here.'

'You're okay, Lucy,' Troy said slowly, 'you're okay.'

It was neither an effusive nor an articulate compliment. But Troy's eyes were smiling at her in a way that made her knees weak, and the sun was dancing on the water as though it didn't have a care in the world. Feeling as though she had traveled a very long way in the last five minutes, Lucy said, 'If we can get everything done that needs to be done before noon tomorrow, we'll both be okay.'

He laughed, his teeth white in his tanned face. 'You said it! I suppose, if I'm to be a skipper worthy of the name, I'd better pass out a few orders.'

'Yessir.'

'I'll take the laundry and the garbage into town, and pick up liquor and drinks. I'll leave you to clean the galley and make up the menus—feel free to repeat anything you served the Merritts.'

'You're not tired of my crab dip?'

'I can always invite Jack over.'

Lucy loved it when he teased her; the sun, if possible, shone even more brightly, and the seagull swooping over the mast was the most graceful bird she'd ever seen. 'I'll need fresh ice for the refrigerator,' she said. With an ingenuousness worthy of Heather she added, 'If you were a really god skipper, with the welfare of your customers truly at heart, you'd go to the spice shop and buy me the second volume of their cookbook series.'

'*Do* you ever cook when you're home, Lucy?'

'I give regular massages to the Italian woman who runs the local pizza shop and to the old Chinese man who has a Szechuan take-out across the street from my apartment.' Her eyes twinkling, she added, 'It's called barter.'

'I suspected you were bluffing the day I hired you,' he said drily. 'You're to be congratulated—the Merritts thought you were a wonderful cook.'

'But then sex gives you an appetite...or so I've heard.'

He let his gaze wander the length of her body in its cotton shorts and brief tank top. 'Only for more sex, I'd suspect.'

Lucy blushed. 'Buy volume two, Troy—for the Dillons' sake.'

When he grinned at her, she suddenly saw another man, young and reckless, clinging to the mast of a Laser in the Strait of Juan de Fuca with the wind tugging at his blond hair. Feeling a lump gather in her throat, she heard him say, 'I promise... I'd better get moving. When I get back, I'll help clean the cabins.'

Five minutes later he was gone. Lucy decided to start by making up menus—a much more difficult task than polishing woodwork or scrubbing out the sinks. Troy had given her the Dillons' list of food preferences. With faint dismay she saw that Brad and Kim favored hamburgers, hot dogs and fried chicken, while their parents wanted poached seafood, salads with low fat dressings and fruit.

Great, she thought. I'll be spending the entire time in the galley. I'd better wait until I get my new cookbook, perhaps that'll inspire me.

When Troy came back, she'd cleaned the cabin that the Merritts had used for storage, and the stove shone like new. She quickly emptied the contents of the freezer so he could store the ice in it, saying, 'I'll do the refrigerator next—I'm going to miss the Merritts more than I thought. The younger Dillons want to wallow in cholesterol and the older ones to eschew it.'

'Volume two,' Troy said, slapping the cookbook on the counter.

Wrinkling her nose at him, she said, 'I should have asked for the whole series.'

'I like your hair like that,' he said unexpectedly. 'You look—lighter somehow.'

I'm falling in love with you, Troy Donovan.

The words had come from nowhere. Her eyes wide with shock, her cheeks washed a delicate pink, Lucy heard them echo and re-echo in her mind. Troy muttered grimly, 'This is going to be one hell of a long five days—or should I say, nights? I'm going to wash out the coolers and put the beer on ice.'

It wasn't the beer he should be putting on ice, she thought numbly.

It was herself. Lucy.

CHAPTER SIX

TROY took the steps two at a time. Her fingers fumbling with the packages of frozen food, Lucy put them back in the freezer and latched the lid, and all the while her thoughts were whirling in crazy circles and her emotions were going up and down as rambunctiously as if *Seawind* were broadside to a swell.

Just because a man compliments you on your hairdo, you don't fall in love with him... But I adore it when his eyes soften and he looks at me as though I'm the only woman in the world... You don't know the first thing about him... I do! I know he's honest and he's hurting... Want to bet that he's still in love with someone else and that's why he's hurting...? He couldn't be so attracted to me if that was the case... That's a laugh. Sex is no basis for falling in love; you're old enough to know that... Oh, shut up!

Which seemed to bring an end to that particular inner dialogue.

Lucy polished the woodwork in the saloon, tidied the books, and went up on deck to shake out the cotton mats that lay on the floor. Then she sat down with the cookbook, scanning the recipes with a more knowledgeable eye than she would have had a week ago. She would have to prepare two meals each evening, that was obvious... Troy could help by barbecuing the hamburgers and chicken. Her pencil flew over the paper, and by the time he joined her she had piled the contents of the refrigerator on the counter and was making notes of what she had to buy.

He made a few entries in the logbook, then filled a pail with suds at the sink, standing so close to her she could have reached out and touched him. Touch... her area of expertise. She said impulsively, 'Troy, when I massaged you yesterday, your muscles were so tight that——'

He turned to face her, his expression far from friendly. 'I suffered through that massage—I already told you that.'

She bit her lip. 'I'm not talking about a superficial kind of tension—this was deep. It felt to me as though you've been carrying a huge weight on your shoulders for a very long time.'

'Stick to menus, Lucy—a much better use for your imagination.'

'I've been giving massages for years—touch is a language I know!'

'Lay off, will you?' he snarled, and swung the pail out of the sink.

How could she ever have thought she was in love with him? She hated his guts! She crammed the food back down into the refrigerator hatch, her mind anywhere but on what she was doing, and twisted to see if she'd left anything out on the counter. Troy was already halfway across the saloon, every inch of his body armored against her. Her eyes glazed with tears. The refrigerator door slipped through her fingers and slammed down on the back of her other hand.

She gave a startled cry of pain, gaping at the heavy wood and metal door that looked as though it had amputated her hand at the wrist. Before she could move, Troy had crossed the cabin, dumped the pail on the counter, and was lifting the door. She pulled her hand free, and as though it belonged to someone else watched it shaking like a leaf in the wind. Small drops of bright red blood appeared from nowhere.

He seized her arm, put her wrist under the cold tap and turned the water on. The blood sheered off in pink sheets. 'Stay there,' Troy ordered. He pulled a first-aid kit out of a lower cupboard, extracted a gauze pad, turned off the tap and pressed the pad to the back of her hand. Then he steered Lucy over to the couch.

'I'm dripping on the floor,' she yelped.

'To hell with the floor!'

'You don't have to polish it,' Lucy said peevishly.

'These islands were the haunts of buccaneers... A bit of blood on the carpet'll add atmosphere to the place. Hold still, Lucy, this might hurt.'

She watched his fingers probe her bruised flesh, marveling at his gentleness. 'Nothing broken,' he said. 'And no need for stitches. But you'll be pretty sore for a couple of days. I'll put on an antibiotic cream and a bandage... and you're going to take it easy the rest of the day. I'll scrub out the bathrooms.'

'All right,' she said meekly. 'At least it's my left hand.'

He glanced up. She was very pale, her skin shadowed blue, her eyes bright with pain. He put down the cream, and with his thumbs slowly traced the curves of bone from her nose to her cheekbones, a gesture of such solicitude that she was touched to the heart. He said, 'We've got to stop this—fighting, I mean.'

'Yes,' she whispered. 'I shouldn't have said anything about the massage. I'm sorry.'

He said, choosing his words as meticulously as if each were a shell he was picking up from the beach, 'Everything you said was true... I'm just not ready to talk about it. Don't take that personally, will you, Lucy? I haven't talked to anyone.'

'I must stop pushing you.' She sighed. 'Although I do wish you'd tell me. Maybe I could help.'

His jaw tightened. 'Some things you can't change.'

It was a strange moment to remember her father, who between one day and the next had disappeared from her life forever. Resting her good hand on Troy's wrist, achingly aware of the jut of bone and the heat of his skin, Lucy said, 'When you're ready, you'll tell someone. And—who knows?—it might even be me.'

He pulled his hand away and said roughly, 'If it were to be anyone, it would be you. I don't have a clue how you do it, but you get past my defences every time.'

'Don't hate me for that,' she pleaded.

'I'll try not to.' His smile a mere movement of his mouth, Troy got up from the couch and brought the first-aid kit over to the table. Ripping open another gauze pad, he added, 'I knew when I hired you I was in for trouble. Knew it the first minute I saw you, when you said you were looking for *Seawind*. Now, hold still.'

The message was clear: he'd had enough of the personal.

Obediently Lucy held still, and equally obediently spent the next hour resting on the deck with a small bottle of juice in her good hand. 'Passionfruit', it was labeled. Not finding this very funny, she drained the bottle, finished her grocery list, and went below deck to polish the brass. If she took her time, her hand didn't hurt too much. Troy had finished the other cabins so she helped wipe the floor and then looked around with pleasure. 'Looks great. What would you like for supper?'

'I'm taking you out for dinner—Caribbean food. For the sake of my blood pressure, wear anything but that sundress. And if you want a shower, why don't you use my cabin? That way these'll stay clean.'

It was the sensible thing to do. But, when Lucy climbed down the ladder into the forward cabin, the shirt Troy had been wearing that morning was flung on his unmade bed, where she could see the indentation his head had made in the pillow. Panic warred with passion in her breast. She had no idea how she was going to get through the next five nights.

The shower was less than satisfactory because she didn't want to get her hand wet; it had been throbbing ever since she had hit it. She dried herself, dressed in her beige trousers with its matching crocheted top over a green silk camisole, and tried to hide the marks of pain with make-up. Her face looked back at her in the little mirror. Troy was right about her hair; the short clustered curls did become her. He's marking me, she thought, with a superstitious shiver of fear, and knew that one lesson she was struggling to learn from him was that of patience.

He had admitted she got through his defences. All she had to do was wait until they fell to the ground.

The restaurant was open to the ocean breeze and charmingly decorated with hibiscus and bougainvillaea; Lucy ate conch patties and flying fish and papaya ice-cream, and at any other time would have been totally happy, sitting across from Troy and watching the moon climb in the sky. But the throbbing in her hand had brought on a throbbing in her temples, and she felt very tired.

Troy called for the bill as soon as they'd finished eating. 'No bar hopping tonight,' he said. 'I'm taking you home.'

Home was *Seawind*. Home was where Troy was. 'I'm sorry—have I been bad company?'

The candle to one side of the table flickered over his features. 'You're the best company there is, and you look worn out.'

She was blushing again. 'I never know what you're going to say next, Troy Donovan.'

'Trade winds are dependable. But maybe a touch boring?'

Lucy chuckled. 'You have yet to bore me.'

He paid the bill, put a casual arm around her waist and steered her toward the Jeep. 'In the morning I'll go with you to do the groceries.'

He wasn't a man for flowery speeches, but he would be there when you needed him, Lucy thought. So in that sense he was like the trade winds. While dependability wasn't the most romantic of concepts, it could be very comforting.

She had never included words like dependability and comfort in her definitions of love before.

She had leaned into his arm, and when they reached the Jeep he put his other arm around her and without a word kissed her parted lips. The palm fronds rustled overhead, and in the bushes the crickets shrilled their monotonous nocturnal song. It was not a passionate embrace, it held none of the anger or desperation that so often had bound them together, but for Lucy it seemed as though another of Troy's defences had fallen—that he had allowed her one step closer to the man he really was.

When they drew apart neither had any need for words. He drove the Jeep to the marina, parked, and they walked arm in arm down the dock to *Seawind*, where the crickets' song was replaced by the metallic keening of the wind in the shrouds. Lucy had left her gear in the saloon, planning to sleep down there that night.

Troy said calmly, 'I'll put your bag in my cabin. When you're in bed, call me and I'll give you a painkiller; it'll help you sleep.'

'But——'

He stilled her protest with a finger on her lips. 'Lucy, I'm only going to say this once. You don't have to be afraid of sharing the cabin with me—I'll wait until you're asleep every night before I go to bed. If we ever make love, I want it to be in a proper bed with no one else on the other side of the wall, have you got that?'

If... The biggest word in the dictionary. Yet even while Lucy's heart was banging against her ribs at the thought of herself and Troy in a proper bed—with or without anyone on the other side of the wall—she also knew she could trust his word implicitly. He would never force himself on her. And, despite their cramped quarters, he would do his best to give her privacy.

'When you're angry with me,' she said unsteadily, 'I can handle you just fine. But when you're like this...I feel like crying—it's ridiculous. I go all mushy inside. Like melted papaya ice-cream—and don't you dare laugh at me. I'm serious.'

'The place for ice-cream that's melting is the freezer.'

'Or else,' she said recklessly, 'it should be eaten as soon as possible.'

Twin sparks flared in his eyes. 'Instead of "if" we make love, I should have said "when"...'

'That's one case where I certainly approve your use of the word "should",' Lucy said, with a lightness that didn't quite succeed.

Troy ran one finger along the soft curve of her lower lip, watching her eyes darken with desire. 'But "when" isn't tonight or the next five nights, Lucy. And, yes, I'm trying to convince myself as much as you.'

'I find that very encouraging,' she remarked.

He laughed, and deliberately stepped away from her. 'I'll put your bag in the cabin. Then you'd better get to bed.'

She watched him leave the saloon. 'When' was a very different word from 'if'. Was she a fool even to think of making love with Troy, a man who in so many ways was an enigma to her? Was this yet another impulsive action that afterwards she would bitterly regret? Troy knew she could only stay in Tortola for four weeks, that she had a job to get back to, an apartment, a circle of friends. So would they make love and then go their separate ways?

She couldn't bear that.

She trailed up the companionway steps, nursing her sore hand, her head pounding. Troy was getting himself a beer from the cooler that was lashed to the lifelines. She edged past him and climbed down into the cabin, where, after switching on the small brass lamp, she cleaned her teeth, undressed, pulled her nightgown over her head and got into bed.

Troy's bunk was perhaps two feet from hers. She gave a violent start as he called down the hatch, 'You ready?'

'Yes,' she croaked, and pulled the sheet up over her breasts as he came down the ladder, his bare feet automatically seeking out the rungs, his long legs moving with supple economy. He went into the bathroom and filled a glass with water. Stooping, he passed it to her and pulled a small vial of pills from the pocket of his shorts. 'One should do,' he said.

She took the white pill from his palm with the very tips of her fingers and swallowed it down. Only wanting him gone, she said, 'Thanks.'

'I'll raise the sails tomorrow—you can take the helm, that'll be easier for you. We'll only go to Norman and Peter Islands, the same as we did with the Merritts.' He smiled at her with impersonal kindness; in the soft light of the lamp his eyes looked almost blue. 'You should feel a lot better tomorrow.'

I love you, Lucy thought blankly. I don't have a choice anymore. I've fallen in love with you whether I want to or not.

'What's the matter?' Troy demanded.

'I—nothing. I'm just tired, that's all.'

She wasn't sure that he believed her. But he straightened, his big body throwing a bigger shadow on the wall. 'I'll see you in the morning,' he said, switched out the light and left the cabin.

Lucy lay down. She could see stars through the open hatch, and found herself remembering Phil. Technically Phil had been the more handsome of the two men. But the only time she'd been ill in the months she'd spent with Phil he'd kept his distance. 'I'll leave the doctoring to your mother,' he'd said with his most charming smile. He'd had lots of charm, she thought, gazing into the darkness. But he hadn't been kind.

In a flash of insight she realized that in his own way he'd been as distant as her mother and her two sisters. Certainly she'd never felt needed by him.

Troy needed her. On that she'd swear.

And she didn't just mean in bed.

When Lucy woke the next morning, rolling over to peer at the alarm clock she kept on her shelf, she bumped her elbow hard against a wooden ledge and sat up with a jerk. She wasn't in her cabin. She was in Troy's.

Her hand hurt.

The digital clock set in the wall said ten to six. Troy was still asleep. Scarcely breathing, Lucy let her eyes wander over him, and, with a deep inner certainty that took her a little further along the road called love, knew that she wanted to wake up beside him every morning for the rest of her life.

She had no experience on which to base this certainty, for her mother had never remarried and her two sisters were too devoted to their careers even to date very much, let alone marry. But she knew it to be true.

His face was turned to her, his thick hair tousled. The sheet had slid to his hips; he was bared to the waist. Even in sleep his fingers were tightly curled into a fist and there was a faint frown furrowing his brow.

Would he ever trust her enough to tell her what was wrong?

It would be so easy to leave her own bunk and crawl into his, to wrap her arms around him so he would wake to the warmth and softness of her body pressed into his. And then what would happen? Would he kiss her and caress her? Would he take off her gown so she was naked to him? Would he feast his eyes on her and let his hands wander to those secret places he had never touched?

He stirred, muttering something under his breath. In a flash Lucy lay down again, feeling the heat scorch her cheeks, a heat that reflected the insidious weakness of desire in her limbs. Troy's breathing slowed and deepened. She closed her eyes, trying to quieten the racing of her pulse, and knew that whatever this big blond man meant to her he was different from the rest.

Twelve hours later the Dillons were seated in the cockpit of *Seawind*, anchored off a quiet cove on Norman Island. Leona Dillon took another cracker spread with crab dip and said languidly, 'Delicious.'

Troy was barbecuing thick hamburgers; Lucy was baking fish with a lime sauce, to be served with wild rice and steamed vegetables. Nursing her left hand, she brought up more nachos and salsa for Brad, who was devouring them as if lunch was a meal that had never happened.

Brad was thirteen; despite his appetite he had yet to remove either his Walkman or his pose of world-weary sophistication. His sister, a year older, had made it clear within five minutes on the boat that she was not here by choice; but the sulky pout of her carmined lips hadn't prevented her from eating her fair share of the nachos, or from casting speculative glances, laced with emergent sexuality, at Troy.

Lucy served dinner in the saloon. She had taken considerable trouble with the meal and was rewarded when Leona asked for the recipe for the lime sauce and Victor cleaned his plate. Leona's simple linen shift would have paid for Lucy's return flight to Ottawa; her hair was a froth of copper curls and her fingernails wouldn't have survived a single turn of the anchor winch. In spite of her glamorous appearance, there was an earthiness to her that Lucy found rather appealing. But if her glamor was for Victor's benefit, Lucy soon realized, Leona was wasting her time.

Ever since he'd come on board, Victor, who was a cardiologist, had had his patrician nose buried in a medical journal. Lucy would have been willing to bet that at home he read while he ate. It had been Victor's decision to anchor in a quiet cove their first night; stubbornness rather than strength of character, Lucy had decided, had ensured he'd gotten his way over the objections of the three other members of his family.

She got up to fetch dessert, a fresh fruit salad along with puff pastries filled with cream and laced with a chocolate fudge frosting. The younger Dillons attacked the pastries, and Leona helped herself and Victor to the salad. Victor eyed the pastries wistfully and dug his spoon into his bowl of fruit.

Resting a predatory hand on Troy's bare arm, Leona said, 'Tomorrow we'll stay at a yacht club, didn't you say?'

'Right... There's a disco there and a steel drum band. A little more action than Norman Island, whose only inhabitants are wild goats and pelicans.'

Leona gave a throaty chuckle. 'Not quite my cup of tea.'

'Troy, will you go with us to the disco?' Kim asked, tossing her hair back with a sultry smile.

Her father interposed, 'He's too old to be courting voluntary deafness, my dear.'

'I'll keep my eye on everyone,' Troy said. 'That's my job.'

'Excellent,' Victor remarked. 'I can catch up on some more reading while you're all ashore.'

Leona sent him a fulminating look and stroked Troy's arm with a provocative smile. 'I'm sure you're a wonderful dancer... a lot of big men are.'

Troy reached for the fruit salad, thereby dislodging her hand. 'You'll have to ask Lucy.'

Thanks a lot, Lucy thought in comical dismay. 'It's no trouble to find someone to dance with, and the band's great.'

'You'll like that, dear,' Victor said to his wife, pushing back his chair. 'If I stay here any longer, I'll succumb to one of those pastries—so I'll go and read for a while.' He gave Lucy a courtly bow. 'An excellent meal, thank you.'

Kim said sulkily, 'I wish there was a TV.'

'There's a bunch of games under the seat. We could play something after dinner,' Lucy suggested.

'Not my style,' Kim complained. 'I miss my boyfriend—he's a fullback on the school team... Although he's not as sexy as you, Troy.'

'Darling!' Leona protested half-heartedly.

'Well, he's not. I like older men.'

'You're so dumb,' her brother remarked, reaching for his Walkman and adjusting the headset.

'I am *not*.' Kim pulled a hideous face at him and flounced up from the table. 'This is going to be the longest five days of my *entire* life,' she declaimed tragically, went to her cabin and slammed the door.

Leona's face settled into lines of discontent that were, Lucy was sure, habitual. 'She needs a man's hand. Victor's always so busy.'

'She needs an overdose,' Brad said, and turned up the volume on his tape.

'Bradley!' Her mouth drooping pathetically, Leona said, 'They're quite out of control—in effect, I'm a single parent. Victor said this was to be a family holiday—and where is he? Reading about lymphocytes and pernicious anemia.'

'Kim is a beautiful girl,' Lucy said diplomatically.

'I had her when I was much too young, of course,' Leona responded, pouting at Troy. 'Silly the things we do when we're teenagers, isn't it?'

Leona was at least forty.

Lucy embarked on a story about some of the more outrageous of her sailing exploits and succeeded in making Leona laugh. After she'd washed the dishes, she suggested that she, Leona and Troy play three-handed bridge; Brad had long since retired to his cabin with his tape collection. When Victor wandered down to the saloon because it was too dark to read in the cockpit, Lucy cajoled him into joining them.

He played with erratic brilliance, as if only part of his mind was on the cards, and then sharp at ten, kissing his wife's cheek, said, 'I like to be up early in the morning. Goodnight, all.'

'And to think I married him because I thought he was fun,' Leona said with a total lack of discretion. 'Kindly don't wake *me* early in the morning.'

The cabin door shut smartly behind her. Troy said softly, for Lucy's ears only, 'The honeymoon's over.'

Lucy smothered a laugh. 'She's unhappy.'

'This is a chartered sloop—not the Love Boat.'

'You shouldn't be such a hunk.'

'Huh. If she'd dug her nails in any more deeply, I'd have bled to death.'

'I'm sure she's only trying to get Victor's attention.'

'Good luck,' said Troy, and put the cards away, yawning. 'We're going to earn our keep this trip, Lucy.'

Nor did the next few days prove him wrong. Troy, by a masterly combination of interest and indifference, got Brad to take the helm, a move that necessitated the removal of the Walkman. And despite his attempts to look bored, it was clear Brad enjoyed steering *Seawind*. Lucy took Kim to every boutique on every island that they passed, and as often as she thought she could get away with it endeavored to separate Victor from his cardiology journals. Leona spent a lot of time lying in the sun on the green mats, in a bikini that wasn't intended to go anywhere near the water.

On their third day they met up with Jack's charter, which included two teenage boys; Kim cheered up appreciably. On the morning of the fourth day they had a near collision with a bareboat captain who had never heard of the rules of the road. Troy's swift avoidance tactics and subsequent tirade at the unhappy skipper of the bareboat shifted Brad from world-weariness to hero-worship, as a result of which he then wanted to learn everything there was to know about sailing before he disembarked. Lucy was amused by his enthusiasm and touched by Troy's patience.

At their lunchtime anchorage Troy somehow managed to get Victor snorkeling, along with Kim and Brad; Lucy, now that her hand had healed, took the opportunity to offer Leona a massage. She worked in silence, bringing all her skill and concentration to play. When she finally sat back on her heels, she said gently, 'There...how does that feel?'

Leona fumbled with the strap of her bikini top and sat up. To Lucy's dismay she saw that Leona was crying, slow tears that leaked between the black fences of her lashes. 'Why doesn't Victor ever touch me like that?' Leona whimpered. 'As though he cares how I feel.' She grabbed for her cosmetic bag, which was never far from her, and took out a tissue. 'I still love him, you see— silly of me, isn't it? I could fight another woman. But medical journals and malfunctioning arteries... I've given up trying to compete with those. I used to flirt with every available man in sight—I even had an affair with a urologist once—and then I tried drinking too much, but all it did was make me sick.' She sighed, dabbing at her cheeks. 'I guess I'm stuck with it. And him.'

Remembering Heather and Craig, Lucy said impulsively, 'Maybe I could teach Victor how to give you a massage.'

'Maybe this boat will sprout wings.'

'I promise I'll try. We've still got all day tomorrow.'

'Honey, I've been married to him for sixteen years— you'll need more than twenty-four hours.'

Lucy was inclined to agree. 'I'd better go. I've got to start supper.'

This time Leona's long scarlet nails rested on Lucy's arm. 'Thanks, Lucy,' Leona said. 'You're a sweetie.'

*   *   *

That evening, as they were all eating Lucy's strawberry mousse, Victor said in his mild voice, 'Ever since we arrived, you've looked familiar to me, Troy. But I can't place you, no matter how hard I try. I've never taken a cruise before, so it's nothing to do with boats. For some reason I associate you with Tennessee—now, why would that be?' He closed his eyes, chewing a whole strawberry ruminatively. 'It's your voice that I remember as much as your face.'

Troy glanced at the journal neatly aligned beside Victor's bowl and said casually, 'I gave a paper at a medical convention in Tennessee two years ago.'

Victor sat up straight, looking as energized as Lucy had seen him. 'Of course! You were the keynote speaker. The latest techniques on skin-grafting—fascinating material.'

As Lucy sat dumbstruck, Leona said speculatively, 'You're a doctor, Troy?'

Victor answered for him. 'An internationally known specialist in craniofacial repair—plastic surgery, my dear. Well, I'm delighted to meet you, Troy. What a pity I didn't speak sooner; we could have had many interesting discussions.'

Leona said bluntly, 'What are you doing this for, Troy?' Her gold bracelets jingling, she indicated the confines of the cabin.

'An old friend of mine runs this charter company. He developed appendicitis with complications and can't come back for another two weeks. I was down here on vacation anyway, so I took over for him.'

'How kind of you,' Leona murmured, running her tongue over her lips as she passed him her wine-glass for a refill; it wasn't an opportune time for Lucy to remember the urologist.

'Quite a change from surgery,' Victor said, looking very pleased with this turn of events.

Lucy got up to plug in the coffee. *She* wasn't pleased. She was, she realized, furious. Troy could tell a group of strangers about his real job but not her, whom he was contemplating taking to bed. From her he'd kept it a secret.

No wonder he'd been so deft at cutting her hair. And how he must have laughed when she'd asked if he was a hairdresser!

With a sickening lurch of her heart she realized something else. His kindness the night she'd hurt her hand had been nothing but his bedside manner: he was being the perfect doctor. After all, a plastic surgeon would deal with women all the time—rich women, who didn't like the effects of aging or who wanted a prettier nose. Women like Leona. She'd been a fool to take it personally.

She wanted nothing more than to throw the remains of the strawberry mousse at the wall. Or at Troy. Instead Lucy arranged the coffee-cups and liqueur glasses on a tray and removed the dessert bowls from the table, smiling pleasantly the whole time. She smiled until her jaw ached, until she was sure an insincere smirk would be plastered to her face for the rest of the cruise. When everyone else went outside to watch the sunset, she stayed below, washing dishes with a ferocious energy that didn't soothe her spirits in the slightest.

She went to bed early, still fuming, and was wide awake when Troy came down the ladder. She should be sensible and lie still, and keep her eyes and her mouth shut. But she didn't feel sensible. She flicked the overhead light on and sat up. And instead of smiling, she glowered at Troy, as if he were a reincarnation of Raymond Blogden.

Not the man with whom she was secretly in love.

CHAPTER SEVEN

TROY was unbuttoning his shirt. 'What's wrong, Lucy?' he said in surprise. 'Can't you sleep?'

'You could write me a prescription for sleeping pills, Dr Donovan,' she said with heavy sarcasm. 'Why didn't you tell me you were a doctor?'

'You didn't ask.'

'Why would I? I assumed you ran the charter and that was your only job.'

'What's the big deal, Lucy? So I'm a doctor, so what?'

Her scowl, if anything, deepened. 'Are there any more little surprises lying in store for me?'

'You're acting as though I'm a drug pusher. Or a heroin addict.'

Lucy sat up straighter in the bunk, her skin gleaming through the lace on her nightgown. 'Let me tell you something. My mother's a forensic pathologist—that's how she met my father; he was one as well, he died when I was three. My elder sister's an immunologist, and my younger sister's an oncologist who's just been awarded a big research grant. I've had it up to here——' she drew her finger theatrically across her throat '—with doctors.'

He flung his shirt across the end of the bed. 'You're stereotyping me again.'

'No, I'm not!'

'Oh, yes, you are. First I'm a big blond hunk and now I'm a doctor. Which other of your prejudices am I going to activate, Lucy?'

'That's a horrible thing to say!'

'When are you ever going to see me as a real person?'

109

The angry retort on the tip of her tongue died away. His question was valid, she thought with painful truth. And she hated it when people misconstrued her own job. Swallowing her pride, she admitted, 'I—I've never felt at home in my family, and a big part of that's related to what they do... So I suppose I am prejudiced against doctors.'

Troy sat down across from her. 'Those specialties you mentioned—they involve very little contact with people.'

She should have realized he'd pick up on that. 'I don't think my family likes people very much.'

'You like people... Why didn't you specialize in family medicine?'

If she'd been smart, Lucy thought, she'd have rehearsed this conversation before embarking on it. 'Because when my parents were handing out the genes for mathematical skills, they skipped me. I can't do physics and chemistry to save my soul. So for three years in a row, to my mother's chagrin, I failed the medical admissions tests. I couldn't even get into physiotherapy, which was my second choice.'

'Does your mother like you?'

Lucy said fretfully, 'Your specialty's plastic surgery. Not psychiatry.'

'So she doesn't... Could it be that you missed out on mathematics but you inherited all the warmth and emotion in your family instead?'

Lucy's eyes filled with sudden tears. 'Is that what you think?' she said in a low voice.

Troy reached out a hand across the gap between their bunks, clasping her wrist. 'Is your family proud of what you do?'

She bent her head. 'Not really. It's not—respectable enough, I guess. And I don't earn nearly as much money as they do.'

'But you like your job.'

'I love it! It's hands-on, it's so direct. I can make people relax and feel better about themselves even in one session. Touch is so important and so neglected nowadays, when either we don't have the time for it or else we sexualize it...' She stared down at his long fingers and added in a rush, 'I've never been turned on by any of my clients—not until you came along.'

He rubbed the little hollow in her wrist with his thumb. 'I'd be willing to bet you threaten the hell out of your mother and your sisters. You've got the courage to go your own way and you love people—I've watched you with Leona. And—you can trust my word on this—you've sure got lots of feelings.'

'*Me* threaten *them*?'

'Yep.'

It was not a point of view Lucy had ever considered before. Yet it made a crazy kind of sense when she thought about it. Feeling as though she'd just made a quantum leap along the steep path to maturity, she muttered, 'No wonder I always feel like a stranger in my own family.'

He was still rubbing her wrist with slow, hypnotic movements. Before she could lose her courage, she blurted, 'Is this just part of your bedside manner?'

He moved over to sit on the edge of her bunk, brought her palm to his lips and kissed it with lingering warmth. 'No,' he said, 'it's because it's your bedside.'

Lucy wasn't entirely convinced. Ever since Victor had spoken she had been aware of an ache of disappointment that Troy had feet of clay. 'You must see a lot of beautiful women, though.'

Troy glanced up, surprised. 'Hardly,' he said.

'But you're a plastic surgeon.'

He frowned at her. 'Did you think I went around doing face lifts and liposuction? Have a heart, Lucy. I deal almost entirely with children. Birth defects and trauma victims. Burns, car accidents—that sort of thing.'

'I'm sorry—I shouldn't have jumped to conclusions,' she said in quick contrition, adding naïvely, 'You must be famous to have been the keynote speaker at that conference.'

He moved his shoulders. 'Oh, well...over the years I've had a few successes.' Playing with her fingers, which were warm against his bare chest, he said huskily, 'The only way I've been able to keep my hands off you the past few nights is because you've been sleeping when I've come to bed.' He shifted restlessly. 'We'd better call it quits right now, or we'll be in trouble.'

'I suppose we should,' said Lucy.

'Your favorite word.' Taking her by the shoulders, he added with an intensity that made her tremble, 'When I came down here last night you were asleep with the moonlight on your face, and with every cell in my body I wanted to possess you... There's nothing I ever read in any medical text on human sexuality that could have prepared me for the way I felt.'

Lucy wanted so badly to tell him she loved him, and could only trust the inner voice that told her to wait, to have patience. 'It's new territory for me, too.'

His voice roughened. 'I own a villa on Virgin Gorda. I usually go there every February and again in April— I'd be there now if Gavin hadn't had his appendix out. We've got two days between the Dillons and the next guests...come to the villa with me, Lucy.'

A proper bed with no one else around. Wasn't that what he had said? 'All right,' she said faintly.

As if her reply had loosened a floodgate, Troy said, 'We'd only have twenty-four hours. But we'd be alone.

The villa can't be reached other than by water, so it's completely private. It's the place I go when I've had too many patients I can't mend the way I want to, and too many parents whose fears I can't allay... Apart from a couple of days at the beginning of this month I haven't been there for nearly a year.'

So was it his job that had built up so much anger and tension in him? He was, after all, only human, and must constantly fall short of what he would wish to achieve for the children in his care. Lucy pushed the hair back from his forehead and smiled into his eyes. 'I'd love to go there.'

'It's my haven,' he said, his words muffled as he brought her fingers to his lips and kissed them one by one. 'In all the years I've owned it, I've never taken a woman there.'

Lucy believed him instantly, and in a rush of joy lifted his face in her hands and kissed him full on the mouth. It was the first time she had taken the initiative so boldly; mixed with joy was the new knowledge of her own power and the rapture of his response, flame leaping to meet flame in the most ancient of burnings.

They kissed for a long time, hungry kisses laced with a passionate tenderness that transported Lucy to a place she'd never been before. It was Troy who finally pulled back, his eyes the dark blue of the ocean depths. He said hoarsely, 'You're like *Seawind* when the wind catches her sails and she leaps to meet the waves... God, how I want you.'

'You shall have me,' Lucy whispered. 'All of me, nothing held back, nothing kept for myself.'

'I've never doubted your generosity.' His face convulsed with longing, Troy kissed her one last time, a deep kiss whose intimacy shivered along Lucy's nerves. 'Goodnight, dearest Lucy.'

I love you, Troy... I love you. While the words, unspoken, illumined her features, from some unacknowledged source of wisdom she said, with just the right touch of lightness, 'Do you think if the cook went on strike the Dillons would go back to Tortola tomorrow instead of the day after?'

His chuckle relieved some of the strain in his face. 'I doubt it—Victor's still got four more journals to read.'

'And Brad wants to learn every nautical term in the book.' She grimaced. 'Breakfast will be at the usual time—provided I get any sleep. Judging by the way I feel right now, that's not too likely.'

'For me, either,' said Troy. He reached up, turned off the light, and moved over to his own bunk.

Lucy curled up, facing him in the darkness. Her body ached to be held by him. But her heart was singing with happiness. Dearest Lucy, she thought. Surely the two most beautiful words in the language.

First thing the next morning Lucy enlisted Troy's help in her campaign to teach Victor massage. 'If you told him about the medical benefits of massage and suggested that he could really help Leona by learning how to do it, he'd pay a lot more attention than if I tried to persuade him. He thinks you're the neatest thing since sliced bread.'

She was brushing her hair in front of the little mirror in the bathroom; Troy was still in bed, propped against his pillow. He said lazily, 'Could it be possible that I'm being used?'

'Very probable, I'd say.'

'You're an unscrupulous woman.'

She grinned at him from the doorway. 'It's all in a good cause.'

'A better cause would be served were you to kiss me good morning.'

'Two kisses if you say yes.'

'Not just unscrupulous. Venal.'

'My true self is emerging,' Lucy said.

'I'll do it. Although I can't imagine that a couple of massage lessons will transform Victor into a model husband.'

It didn't seem very likely to Lucy, either. 'I have to try, though,' she said. 'For Leona's sake.'

Troy gave his rare smile. 'You're a nice person, Lucy Barnes.' His eyes darkening, he added, 'Come here. There's a small matter of two kisses. Whose duration you neglected to specify.'

'Clearly I need lessons in venality,' she said, and felt her heart begin to race as she approached his bunk.

Two kisses, she soon learned, could last quite a long time. She was pink-cheeked when she headed for the galley, and forgot to put nutmeg in the French toast. She served it with sausages, maple syrup and hot applesauce, and afterward was amused at how neatly Troy commandeered Victor for a talk up by the bow.

Troy then took Kim and Brad snorkeling, promising Brad a barracuda and Kim an angelfish. Victor, looking as though he was about to perform his first major operation, consented to be shown the techniques of a back and shoulder massage. Lucy did her best with the two of them, neither of whom was at all relaxed, and did at least leave them after the session sitting together on the green mat talking to one another.

Troy, Brad and Kim were chugging back in the dinghy. The first moment they were alone, Troy asked, 'How did it go?'

'For a cardiologist,' Lucy answered drily, 'Victor knows almost nothing about matters of the heart.'

'One more doctor out of touch with his feelings,' Troy said.

He had spoken with an underlying bitterness that made it seem more and more likely to Lucy that his job was the source of his unhappiness. Tucking this thought away for future reference, she said, 'Lesson two is tomorrow morning, before we dock.'

'And then,' said Troy, 'we'll head for the villa.'

Heat scorched Lucy's cheeks. She was standing on the opposite side of the cockpit to Troy, but she felt bound to him as surely as if they were locked in each other's arms. 'I'll go and lift the anchor,' she mumbled, and turned away, then saw Leona stationed at the forepeak watching them.

'Privacy is beginning to seem a most desirable commodity,' she added between gritted teeth.

That day Brad took the helm every chance he got, Kim and Leona went shopping in Spanish Town, and Victor thereby was able to read two more journals in peace and quiet. Everyone was happy, thought Lucy, amazed that with all this activity the hours could creep by so slowly.

One moment she longed for it to be midday tomorrow, the next she was plunged into a cold sweat. Because she loved Troy, making love with him seemed both inevitable and right. But, because Troy had given no indication that he loved her, she was also afraid. She already knew that going to bed with him would make her vulnerable as she had never been before.

They would have, at the most, twenty-four hours at the villa. And then what?

Late that afternoon Lucy had the galley to herself. Jack's charter had joined them at the anchorage, so Brad and Kim were swimming with the teenagers in Jack's party;

Victor had gone for a sleep in his cabin and Leona was sunbathing on the deck. Troy had taken the dinghy to Spanish Town on an unexplained errand. Humming to herself, she had put the last touches to a chocolate cheesecake and was mixing herbs for wild rice when Leona descended the stairs.

After pouring herself a rum and Coke, Leona sat in the nearest swivel chair and said, 'I don't know how you persuaded Victor into that lesson—but thank you, Lucy.'

Lucy wasn't about to divulge the part Troy had played. 'Tomorrow—same time, same place,' she said, measuring water into a saucepan for the rice.

Leona leaned forward. 'You and Troy looked just like Kathleen Turner and Michael Douglas this morning... You know what I mean? Sort of sizzling.'

'Too much tropic sun,' Lucy said feebly.

'Who are you kidding?' said Leona. 'You looked like you belonged together. Like you were in love.'

'Then appearances are deceptive.'

'Hey, he's gorgeous. Most women, if a guy like Troy looked at them like that, would be out trying on wedding dresses. I know you're both single—I asked him that the first day we were on board—so what's the hold up?'

Leona was only a third through her rum, and Lucy was trapped in the galley. But after tomorrow, she'd never see the Dillon family again. Busily arranging sliced almonds on a tray to toast them, she confessed, 'Ever since I was in grade seven, the only kind of man I ever fell in love with was big, blond and handsome. Like Troy. But either I fall out of love or the man doesn't hang around long enough for me to do so. I was engaged once—he upped and left me. My track record, in other words, is lousy.'

'Troy doesn't look the type to take off.'

'Maybe it's my own feelings I'm scared to trust.'

'You've never been attracted to Burt Reynolds or Mel Gibson or Tom Hanks?'

Lucy shook her head. 'But I'm a pushover for Robert Redford and Nick Nolte.'

Leona's eyes narrowed. She took a long, thoughtful sip of her rum. 'What colour's your father's hair?'

'My father?' Lucy repeated, puzzled. 'My father died when I was three.'

'Oh, sorry—I didn't know that . . . But I dare say he still had hair. In fact, if he died young, he probably had a full head of it. What colour was it, Lucy?'

Lucy gripped the edge of the counter. The most vivid memory of her early childhood, and almost her only memory of her father, was of herself being thrown high in the air—so high that she was surrounded by apple blossoms, pink and white against a blue sky—and then caught by giant of a man whose blond hair gleamed like gold in the sunlight. He had been laughing, she remembered. Laughing and handsome and vibrantly alive.

'Blond,' she said numbly.

'I knew it!' Leona crowed. 'My analyst told me that you're always attracted to men like your father. You often marry them. Which might well account for the divorce rates,' she finished cynically.

Stunned, Lucy stood still. Her father, her big, blond, handsome father, had walked out of the house one day and never come back. A heart attack, her mother had told her years later. And she, Lucy, had been subconsciously searching for him ever since. Falling in love over and over again with men like him, men who often deserted her—just as her father had left the little girl he had played with in the orchard.

She knew Leona was right; knew it in her bones. She also knew that she was going to cry. She said incoherently, 'I—I've got to—— Excuse me, Leona,' and fumbled her way out of the galley and up the steps.

Troy was just climbing out of the dinghy. Averting her head, she clambered over the bench and scrambled forward, praying he wouldn't follow her. She almost fell down the ladder into their cabin. Flinging herself down on the bed, she stuffed her face into her pillow to muffle the sobs that were crowding their way from her throat.

Then she was being half lifted, and through a curtain of tears saw that it was Troy. Big, blond Troy. She could hear herself crying—thin, high sounds like an animal in pain. 'G-go away,' she wept, and felt him gather her into his arms and press her to his chest. He was warm and solid and very much alive; she sobbed all the harder, her fists clutching his shirtfront, her forehead hard against his breastbone.

He held her until she had cried herself out. Only then did he wipe her wet cheeks with a handful of tissues, waiting until she had blown her nose before he said, 'Lucy, dear, what's the matter?'

She scrubbed at her face with the back of her hand, her breath catching in her throat. For a moment she closed her eyes, wrapping her arms around him so tightly that he added, in mixed amusement and concern, 'I'm not going to go away. Just tell me what's wrong.'

'This is going to sound so silly,' she gulped. 'You see, I was crying for my father.'

'Your *father*? But he died years ago.'

'I know.' Lucy drew a couple of deep breaths and looked up at Troy, her nose splotchy, her eyes still swimming with tears; she desperately wanted him to understand. 'I don't think I've ever cried for him before. He vanished when I was three—I don't remember going to the funeral, and it was years afterward that my mother told me he'd had a massive coronary. When Leona and

I were talking a few minutes ago...it suddenly hit me like a ton of bricks that I've been looking for him all my life. He was a big, blond, handsome man, you see.' She blew her nose again and stumbled on, 'It sounds corny, and I'm not trying to excuse myself...but I know that's why I kept falling in love with big blond men—I couldn't help it.'

Troy said warily, 'There's a certain logic to that.'

'I feel as though I've been in a cage all my life without even knowing it, and I've suddenly been given the key. Because I won't have to do that anymore. Troy, don't you understand? I can fall in love with whom I please.'

'I see,' he said, in a voice empty of emotion.

She hurried on before she could lose her courage, 'If I ever saw you as my father, I'm truly sorry. I know it won't happen again. You're you. Troy. Who happens to be big and blond and handsome.' Her smile was as dazzling as sun after rain. 'How could I have been so blind all these years? It seems so obvious now—about my father, I mean. Anyway, what I'm really saying is that I'm free to see you exactly as you are. For yourself.'

She seemed to have run out of words. Troy said, 'So you're not planning to fall in love with the first black-haired man you meet?'

'I'm planning to go to the villa with you tomorrow,' Lucy said steadily. 'If you still want me.'

'Oh, yes, I still want you.'

Aware of undercurrents, but having no idea of their nature, she added ruefully, 'Pretty silly to be crying for a man who's been dead for twenty-two years. I've heard of people delaying grief, but never to that extent, have you?'

'Not to that extent, no,' he said with careful precision.

'Is anything wrong, Troy?' She searched his face, finding nothing there but the guardedness that she had almost come to expect.

'Of course not,' he said shortly. 'Maybe you'd better go and find Leona. She looked rather as though she'd rubbed the magic lamp and an unexpectedly awesome genie had emerged.'

The words tripped from Lucy's tongue. 'Did you have a patient recently who died because of a heart attack?'

'No, Lucy. Off you go.'

His face was closed against her. Lucy got to her feet, washed her face in the bathroom and came back into the bedroom. She said evenly, 'Dinner's going to be late.'

'Doesn't matter. After dinner I thought we'd go ashore for a while. They're playing calypso music at the club, and Jack's lot will be there as well.'

Lucy felt more like going to sleep than going ashore. She climbed the ladder, went aft and found Leona in the cockpit, nursing what looked like the same glass of rum and Coke. Before the other woman could speak, Lucy said in a rush, 'I'm sorry I ran out on you like that—I've just cried my eyes out for a man who's been dead for over twenty years. Because you were right, Leona—I've been searching for him ever since he died, and thank goodness I didn't marry the big blond man I was engaged to a couple of years ago.' Impetuously she stepped closer and hugged Leona. 'Thanks,' she said. 'You changed my life by saying what you said.'

'I *did*?'

'Truly,' Lucy said with a watery grin.

'Wow,' said Leona. 'You know what? Victor and I had the best—well, let's be honest—the *only* talk we've had in months after that massage.'

'So if dinner's a bit of a flop, it's been worth it?'

'You bet! Give me something to do and I'll help get dinner on the table.'

Lucy had no idea if it was against the rules for the guests to help the cook, but Leona looked more animated than Lucy had seen her, and Lucy wasn't about to quench that animation. 'Let's go,' she said.

The *pièce de résistance* of the meal was bananas *flambé*, the dark rum sending blue flames dancing over the fruit. They ate by candlelight—Lucy hoping to disguise the marks of her crying spell—and Troy plied the adults with wine; Lucy washed the dishes in a pleasant haze.

As she put away the last of the cutlery, she knew she'd told the truth to Leona: the insight about her father had indeed liberated her from a destructive pattern of many years. Paradoxically she felt much closer to the man who had fathered her. Troy had also shifted in her vision. She still loved the way the candle flames glimmered through his thick streaked hair, loved the breadth of his shoulders, the length of his legs. The play of muscles in his forearms kindled in her a fierce flame of desire, and the strong bones of his face, with its impenetrable slate-blue eyes and jutting cheekbones, drew her to him as the flowers of the hibiscus opened to the sun. He was blond, big and handsome; that hadn't changed. But she loved him because he was Troy. And every breath she drew told her that this time her love wouldn't alter. This was forever.

With a little jolt she saw that he had come back to the saloon and was standing watching her. He'd changed into a blue shirt and off-white cotton trousers, his untidy hair combed to a semblance of order. His eyes were indeed impenetrable, she thought with a tiny shudder of unease. But all he said was, 'Can you be ready in five minutes, Lucy? The others are waiting.'

Twenty-four hours from now, what would she and Troy be doing?

Lucy said breathlessly, 'Sure,' and ran past him up the stairs. In the cabin she pulled on her sundress, hastily made up her face and daubed herself with perfume. Her eyes were very bright in the little mirror.

She was the last one to get in the dinghy. Kim was dressed to the hilt, because Jack's guests were going dancing as well; Brad sported a T-shirt with sailboats on front and back and a nautical cap. On shore the lanterns strung between the palm trees beckoned like multi-colored stars.

Troy and Jack pulled tables together so everyone could get to know each other, and even though her emotions felt about as stable as *Seawind* in a hurricane, Lucy coped valiantly with too many strangers and too much con-viviality. She drank her fair share of rum punches, danced with every man at the table except Troy, and was somehow not at all surprised to find that he had disappeared when she came back to the table after five minutes of dodging Jack's leaden feet.

She switched to Coke, danced some more, and suddenly decided she too had had enough. Slipping between the tables, she headed toward the beach along a narrow dirt path that wound between the palms. To her overwrought imagination the fronds looked like unsheathed bayonets; sharp-edged, they clattered in the wind. When she reached the sand, she slipped off her sandals and walked barefoot, glad to be alone.

Mangroves had sculpted the beach into a series of curves, each hidden from the rest, some sandy, some piled with rocks and chunks of coral; imperceptibly Lucy began to relax. She was almost ready to head back to the dance-floor when she caught a new sound over the soft ripple of the waves and the susurration of the palms:

a heavy rattle, as though the rocks were being disturbed. It would take something very large to make that much noise, she thought, her nerves tightening. There it was again.

She was tempted to rejoin the crowds at the club, her ears still able to catch the distant lilt of the music, but she hadn't arrived in these enchanted islands by playing it safe. She could creep closer in the shelter of the trees, just to see what it was. Goats, probably. Or a wandering donkey. They were loose everywhere.

Although it didn't seem too likely that a donkey would be interested in rocks and coral.

As she edged nearer, until the next strip of beach came in sight, she had enough caution to stay hidden behind the thick leaves of a sea-grape shrub. The noise hadn't been caused by donkeys or goats, she saw at once. And recognized immediately the man balanced on the rubble in his light trousers and darker shirt. Even as she watched he picked up a rock, and with concentrated fury threw it hard against a huge boulder.

In a young boy this might have been seen as a game. But for Troy it was in deathly earnest. Now that she was closer Lucy could hear the harsh intake of his breathing, almost like a sobbing in his throat. He bent, again hefting a chunk of rock in his hand, then flung it at the boulder, his feet braced in the jumble of coral. The explosion of sound made Lucy shudder. She shrank back behind the shrub.

His rage, so inarticulate, so ferocious, came as no surprise. She had lived with it for the last two weeks. She had seen it erupt into violence in the stucco villa that belonged to Raymond Blogden. It had kept her at arms' length from a man whom, foolishly or not, she had grown to love. Even now, she knew she lacked the courage to confront him.

The job hadn't been invented that could have brought him to such a pitch of rage; she was sure of that. A woman. It had to be a woman. The first day she'd met him he'd warned her off. 'No male-female stuff,' he'd said. Why warn her if he hadn't been hurt, left so badly scarred that he was reduced to working off his anger on a lonely beach the only way he knew how? Any jealousy that Lucy had felt before was nothing compared to the ugly turmoil in her breast now; how intimate he must have been with this unknown woman; how much love he must have felt for her!

She jumped as the crack of rock on rock once more shattered the peace of the tropic night. He should have been dressed all in black, she thought wildly, for he was a man of darkness, a keeper of secrets. She was afraid of the force of his anger. Afraid of finding out about his past.

She might be frightened, but she was aware, too, that Troy had walked the length of several beaches in order to find privacy, that whatever demons he was trying to exorcise were his, and his alone, and that he wouldn't thank her for intruding.

She couldn't help him. She didn't know how.

Was this also love? This painful recognition that she was helpless? That all she could offer Troy was a silent prayer from the depths of her heart, and the solitude that he needed?

Like a gunshot, a hunk of dead coral struck the boulder. In the echoing silence she heard Troy's breath hiss between his teeth. Lucy turned around, torn by conflicting emotions, and hurried back along the beach. Maybe she was making the biggest mistake of her life to leave him... Did he really need solitude, or did he, unknown to himself, need the comfort of another human being? Was it respect for his struggle that had made her turn her back on him, or was it cowardice?

This was the man who was going to be her only companion in a lonely villa for twenty-four hours. Was she crazy? Or would he choose the villa, his haven, to tell her about the woman who had wounded him so grievously?

With no answers for any of her questions, Lucy ran along the dirt path toward the lights and music of the club. A huge part of her simply wanted to wrap her arms around the nearest palm tree and cry her eyes out. For the second time that day.

Was love inseparable from tears?

No one seemed to have noticed Lucy's absence; she slipped back into her seat and within moments was asked to dance by one of the more raucous of Jack's guests. Although she threw herself into the music, her skirt whirling about her knees, her hips gyrating, the ache in her heart didn't go away, and her eyes were constantly on the look out for Troy. When she went back to her seat, Victor rather ponderously asked her to dance. He was wearing a Hawaiian flowered shirt that Lucy was sure Leona had bought for him and he led her round the dance-floor with a flair she wouldn't have expected of him.

'Are you having a good time, Victor?' she asked.

'Well, yes,' he said, sounding rather surprised that this should be so.

Troy still hadn't come back, and perhaps it was this—along with two rum punches and a day that had been far from ordinary—that made Lucy say with conscious provocation, 'You know, Victor, you have a wife who really loves you—don't blow it, will you?'

He missed a step. 'I beg your pardon?'

'Troy would fire me if he knew I was speaking to you like this,' she said, giving him the benefit of her most ravishing smile, 'but there's more to life than a stack of cardiology journals.'

'I enjoy reading them,' Victor said stiffly. 'It's only on holiday that I have the time.'

'Just as there's more to the heart than a bunch of valves.'

With a touch of humour that greatly encouraged her, Victor replied, 'Certainly that statement would be regarded as scientifically correct.'

'It's never a good idea to take a woman for granted,' Lucy persisted, exactly as if she knew what she was talking about. 'Leona's a sweetheart, and how long is it since you told her you loved her? Oh, lord, there's Troy. I'm going to shut up.'

'You are,' said Victor, 'a rather remarkable young woman.' And he steered her back to the table.

Remarkable could be interpreted any number of ways, not all of them flattering, Lucy thought, and sat down next to Troy. Victor or Leona would probably see nothing different about him; she, who knew him in ways she didn't fully understand, saw the bruised shadows under his eyes and a nasty scrape on his knuckles that hadn't been there earlier in the day. She said lightly, 'Dance with me, Troy?'

For a moment she thought he was going to refuse. Then he pushed back his chair and led her out on to the floor. Before he could reach out for her, she laced her hands around his neck, pressed her body to his and began to sway to the music. 'That's better,' she said softly. 'I needed this.'

She felt his hands slide past her waist to her hips, then one palm stroked its way up her spine to rest on the bare flesh of her back. His cheek was resting on her hair, and she knew she had been craving to be held by him ever since she had seen him on the beach. She had no need for words, letting her body do the talking for her in its surrender and its warmth.

She was no closer to knowing what Troy had been wrestling with on the beach but she did sense that the struggle had exhausted him, and that he, like her, simply wanted the intimacy of this silent embrace. She could have wished the music to last forever. When it eventually ended, Troy led her away from the other couples into a dark corner and murmured, keeping his arms around her, 'This is not what my mother intended me to learn when she sent me at the age of eleven to dance camp.'

'*I* like it,' said Lucy.

'I need so badly to have you to myself,' he muttered, and tightened his hold.

And what could she add to that? I love you, seemed the only answer. Yet they were three words she still wasn't ready to say.

Or he to hear.

CHAPTER EIGHT

PROMPTLY at noon the next day the Dillons stepped on to the dock in Road Town. Troy had taught Brad how to jibe that morning, and furnished him with a list of sailing schools; Victor had been given a second lesson in massage, and had finished reading his pile of journals, while Kim had presented Lucy with one of her favorite tapes. Leona, before disembarking, had hugged Lucy and said, a little too loudly for Lucy's taste, 'Don't forget what I said about wedding dresses.'

Lucy waved until they were out of sight. It seemed a lifetime ago that she had done the same thing with the Merritts. Heather had also made a remark about weddings.

She turned back to Troy. He said tersely, 'Let's get out of here before anything happens to delay us. We'll do all the housekeeping stuff when we get back tomorrow.'

They wouldn't even have a full day at the villa, Lucy thought as she went forward to hoist the anchor; they'd have to be here tomorrow afternoon to clean and re-provision the boat. She was beginning to develop a healthy respect for the skippers and crews of the chartered yachts that plied the harbor.

Once the sails were hoisted and trimmed, she went below and made sandwiches for lunch. As wind and waves worked their usual magic she began to relax, all the more so because *Seawind* was making a steady nine to ten knots and they were soon in sight of the shores of Virgin Gorda. It seemed a good omen when Troy

129

pointed out a pair of tropic birds, their bills red as the blooms on the hibiscus, their slim, elegant bodies trailing long white plumes.

'They nest in the rocks along the coast every year,' he said, smiling at her in uncomplicated pleasure. He was slouched at the wheel, steering with one foot. He looked happy, she thought, and smiled back.

His villa was all she could have wished. They anchored off a narrow crescent of pure white sand, where the water was the clear turquoise of a gemstone. Once they'd put a few personal belongings in the dinghy they went ashore, lifting the dinghy well up on the beach. A path edged with rocks wound up a slope through a grove of coconut palms, widening into a garden that was a blaze of color.

Lucy stopped in her tracks. There were the usual tall bushes of scarlet hibiscus, but there were golden ones as well, and gorgeous white ones with vermilion centers. A frangipani tree, it's blooms a deep waxy pink, filled the air with scent. Yellow and red poinciana, purple wreath vine, white spider lilies, the gaudy fuchsia of bougainvillaea ... 'I feel as though I'm in a hothouse,' she marveled. 'Troy, it's beautiful! But who looks after it when you're not here?'

'Friends of mine live here ten months of the year, and do the upkeep in return. I have a thirty-foot ketch that they look after, too.'

A tiny hummingbird, its feathers flashing emerald fire, zipped past Lucy's nose, and from the woods she heard the soft cooing of doves. Troy led the way to the house, which was built of stone and stucco; the deck was shaded by latticework hung with vines, some with yellow trumpet-shaped flowers, others with plumes of mauve blossoms that quivered in the wind. A hammock was slung between two of the posts. Before she went inside,

Lucy rested her hands on the railing, looking out over the water. 'I see why you love it here,' she said.

'Come and see the inside.'

Tile floors, pastel walls and wicker furniture gave a sense of coolness and space to the interior. There were a few exquisite watercolors of local scenes, while the plants that softened the corners of the rooms were glossy with health. Lucy had more than enough imagination to have filled in the gaps in Troy's job description; he would need a retreat, a place where beauty was effortless and no demands would be made on him. And here he had such a place, she thought, knowing that the last few minutes had furnished a few more pieces to the puzzle that was Troy. She said spontaneously, 'Thank you for inviting me here.'

'My pleasure. Want to go for a swim?'

She wasn't sure what she wanted. For a man who more than once had professed his desperate need of her, Troy seemed in no hurry to take advantage of the fact that they were finally alone together. He had put her bag in the white-painted bedroom, where a cool green spread decorated a bed that looked intimidatingly large, but he had made no effort to entice her into that bed. Didn't he want to make love to her anymore? Wishing she were not so conscious of how little time they had, she said, 'A swim would be lovely.'

And so it was. They shared the water with a pair of pelicans and a sleek brown booby, whose antics more than made up for any lack of conversation between Troy and Lucy. Then they wandered back up to the house, Lucy wondering why her bikini, which earlier had had such a satisfactory effect on him, now seemed to have none at all. 'There's a shower off the bedroom,' Troy said casually, 'why don't you use that one and I'll take the main bathroom? Then I'll pour you a drink.'

And after that it would be time to start dinner, she thought, and more of their precious time would have slipped past. Perhaps she had totally misinterpreted him. He hadn't wanted her as much as he'd wanted to be here in this enchanting retreat.

She closed the bedroom door behind her and looked around. The only photograph in the room rested on a set of bamboo bookshelves; its expensive gold frame surrounded a color print of an elderly couple standing against a background of fir trees. The man, who had an untidy of silver hair, had Troy's chin and strong cheekbones, while the woman, smaller, neater, had her son's gray eyes. This was the couple who considered strong feelings in bad taste, Lucy remembered, knowing she was looking at Troy's parents. He'd never mentioned any sisters or brothers; from the lack of any other photos she assumed he must have been an only child. A fig tree overhung a writing desk by one of the windows. The watercolor over the bed was of a crowded back-street in Road Town, alive with people and cars and flowering trees, vines rampaging over the old buildings with their colorful wooden shutters. The bedroom, so cool and uncluttered as to be almost monastic, needed that painting.

As she went into the bathroom something else caught her eye. Pinned to the wall of the little hallway was a boldly printed scarf. Lucy had seen these in the boutiques she had visited with Kim, and had regretfully decided they were beyond her pocketbook. They were made to be worn as sarongs, draping the body in any number of ways. This one was emerald-green, turquoise and red, reminding her of the hummingbird, of the sea where she had swum with Troy and of the hibiscus blooms nodding outside the bedroom windows.

Her bag contained a clean pair of shorts and a matching top, her sundress, and a nightgown that had not been bought with seduction in mind. Impulsively she loosened the pins, taking the scarf down and shaking it out. Going into the bathroom, she draped it over her bikini, where the bright hues brought out the blue in her eyes. Throwing it over the towel rail, she showered the salt from her hair and body.

Still wrapped in the towel, she went out on the deck leading from the bedroom and plucked a hibiscus flower, which she pinned into her hair in front of the bathroom mirror; this was a maneuver not as easy to accomplish as movie heroines might have had her believe. By the time she was finished her cheeks were flushed and her eyes wide with a mixture of emotions she was not about to categorize. The hibiscus, she had long ago decided, was a very erotic flower, and was she not doing her best to seduce Troy?

She spent several more minutes draping herself in the scarf. She didn't have the nerve to wear it around her hips with the rest of her body bare, and she didn't want to put her bikini top back on; it was too wet. So she compromised, by tucking the fabric low over her breasts. For reasons she couldn't fully have explained, this didn't seem the time or the place for make-up, perfume or jewellery. She wanted Troy to see her as she was. No more, no less.

The bedroom had a full-length mirror. The woman reflected in it was almost a stranger to her. Because the fabric was opaque, her skin glowed through it. It only covered her to mid-thigh; her legs looked impossibly long. In a panic she reached for her bag, to take out her sundress and pull it on, and heard Troy call, 'Lucy, are you all right?'

'I'll be out in a minute,' she quavered.

If Troy no longer wanted to be seduced, she was about to make a total fool of herself. She had to believe he hadn't changed, that he wasn't Phil or any of the other big, blond men who had briefly peopled her past. That his hunger for her was real and lasting, rooted in his integrity. He had never said he loved her, but he had never brought any other woman except herself to this place that was so close to his heart, either.

Calling on all her training, Lucy tried to relax. Then she opened the door and walked to the living-room, the tiles cold under her bare feet. Troy was standing with his back to her on the deck, looking out over the water. She pushed the screen to one side and stepped out into the open air.

As he turned to face her, he said, 'I was getting worried about—— My God, Lucy.'

The breeze had flattened the sarong to her body, faithfully tracing the fullness of her breasts and her flat belly, the fabric revealing more than it concealed. The dappled sunlight patterned her bare shoulders and the slim length of her legs; her eyes, wide-held, were the gray blue of an ocean storm.

Lucy clutched the railing, her mouth dry, wishing she had opted for her sundress, wishing he would say something, but quite unable to think of anything to say herself. She should have been striking some kind of voluptuous pose, she thought frantically. She should be gazing at him through lowered lashes with her lips pouting. Instead of which she was frozen to the deck, paralyzed like a frightened rabbit. And about as alluring.

'I—I'll go and change,' she stammered, and backed up a step.

'Don't go!' He put his drink down on the weathered teak table and crossed the deck, stopping three or four feet away from her. 'You're very brave,' he said with a crooked smile.

'Or a lunatic.'

'You don't have to be afraid...'

'I'm scared witless,' Lucy said, and felt a little of her fear lift with the simple act of speaking the truth.

His hair was still damp from the shower; he was wearing a white T-shirt that molded his body like a second skin and a pair of denim shorts. Hoping he would take her in his arms, she watched him shove his hands in his pockets instead. He said roughly, 'I know I'm not handling this well—I'm sorry... You see, this house has always been an escape for me. From the realities of a job where I can so rarely do enough. Where all my skills of hand and brain aren't sufficient to heal the kids in my care the way I'd like to heal them. Then, on top of that, I've been stuck in a—a bad personal situation for a long time... too long. So I wanted this to be time out.' He hit his fist on the railing, making her jump. 'Dammit! It sounds like I'm talking about a hockey game instead of a romantic tryst—I wouldn't blame you if you told me to get lost.'

The same tumult of emotion that had held her paralyzed was twisting his mouth in an ugly grimace, and somehow this emboldened her to speak. 'I'm not going to do that. Not if you don't want me to.'

His short laugh had little humor in it. 'I want you here more than I can say.' Raking his fingers through his hair, he went on raggedly, 'I need peace and quiet. I need to lose myself in you, Lucy. Maybe that way I'll find myself again, I don't know.' He looked straight at her. 'I do realize I have no right to ask this of you.'

Lucy stood taller, her fear dropping from her as swiftly as if she had loosened the scarf to let it fall to the floor. Troy was a proud man, a man not used to speaking of his feelings; that he had revealed his needs to her was a nakedness at least as powerful, if not more so, than that of the body. She said, and it was the absolute truth, 'You may ask of me whatever you wish.'

'I don't know what I did to deserve you,' he muttered.

'I could say the same for myself.' Her smile faded. 'I was afraid I'd misread all the signals, that you didn't bring me here to make love to me after all. But you'd tell me if that was the case, wouldn't you? You see, Phil didn't tell me he'd fallen for Sarah for well over a month, and when I found out I was so humiliated. I loathe deception! Even if the truth hurts, I'd rather know what's going on than be kept in the dark.'

'Oh, Lucy,' Troy said, closing the distance between them and resting his hands on her bare shoulders. 'Beautiful Lucy...' His smile was rueful. 'The truth is that when I went to Spanish Town I went to the drugstore so I'd be prepared if we did make love. That's not very romantic, either, is it? But at work I so often see children that aren't wanted, and that suffer in consequence.' He paused, his face intent on hers. 'If you and I were ever to bring a child into the world, it would be because we both chose to do so.'

Was this Troy's way of saying he loved her? Lucy didn't know. She did know that the thought of bearing his child filled her with a bittersweet happiness. She and Troy had never talked of the future, of the time beyond the four weeks for which he had hired her; perhaps here, in this place, he would do so.

'Never think that I don't want you,' he added forcibly. 'If I'd followed my instincts, I'd have torn the clothes off you and ravished you on the sand before we'd even hauled the dinghy up on the beach. But—quite apart from the physical difficulties of making love on a beach—I didn't want to fall on you as though I was starving. I didn't want to rush you.'

Finally Lucy did what she'd wanted to do when she had first walked out on the deck. She reached forward, pulled Troy's T-shirt free of the waistband of his shorts, and slid her palms up his bare chest, tangling her fingers in his body hair. 'I don't feel the slightest bit rushed,' she said.

Her lips had curved in an enticing smile. With an inarticulate sound of gratification and passionate hunger, Troy pulled her closer and kissed her, teasing her lips apart, tasting all the sweetness of her mouth. Her sarong slipped a little.

Laughter warming her voice, Lucy said, 'Can they see us from the water? If you keep that up, I'm going to be stark naked.'

Troy glanced seaward, where two yachts were cruising the coastline. 'I'm not into sharing you . . . even long-distance,' he said. 'Let's go inside.' As she eased her hands free of his shirt, he added, letting his gaze wander down her body, 'Why is it that flesh showing through clothing is so erotic?'

Lucy blushed. Before she could move Troy had swung her up into his arms. Linking her fingers around his neck, she teased, 'You made that look awfully easy—I'm impressed.'

'Hey, I'm tough,' he rejoined. 'I knew there had to be a reason I lifted weights all last winter. Can you close the screen? Or the geckos will get in.'

'Lizards in my bed don't turn me on,' Lucy said primly.

He had reached the bedroom door. 'Are you going to tell me what turns you on in bed, Lucy Barnes? Or are you going to let me find out for myself?'

'That's easy,' she said breathlessly, as he put her down beside the bed and pulled back the covers. 'You turn me on, Troy Donovan. You don't have to do a darn thing.'

'You mean if I do this——' he stroked the rise of her breast from her cleavage to her nipple, cupping it in his hand and watching her face '—it doesn't do anything for you?'

'Amend that last statement,' she said weakly. 'Everything you do turns me on.'

His answer was to kiss her again, a slow, tantalizing kiss that spread heat through her limbs like a tropic sun. She kissed him back, exulting in the flick of his tongue and the passionate single-mindedness with which he was besieging her.

She was clutching him round the waist. When he raised his head and started removing the hibiscus from her hair, she murmured 'You've got too many clothes on.'

'Complaining already, huh?'

'Suggestions for improvement are not the same as complaints.'

'In that case . . .' He stripped the T-shirt off, dropping it on the floor.

Lucy began to laugh, a delicious cascade of sound. 'I don't think I've ever been happier in my whole life than to be here with you, Troy,' she said. His face softened, and mixed with her laughter was a shaft of joy that, for now, she had made him forget the demons that drove him.

Taking her face in his hands, he said, 'You're a lovely woman, Lucy . . . beautiful in all ways.'

'Thank you,' she whispered.

His voice deepened. 'We could improve the situation still further, don't you think?' In a swift movement he pulled off his shorts and tossed them to the floor, so that for the first time she saw him naked.

If she'd had any doubts that he wanted her, she needed have none now. Her cheeks as red as the flower he had put on the bedside table, she said, 'You're beautiful, too,' and reached for the top of her sarong.

He stayed her hands. 'Let me.' He kissed her again. Then he was trailing kisses down her throat and along the arch of her collarbone, all the while loosening the sarong. When it slipped down to her waist his mouth followed it, exploring the silken valley between her breasts and the firm rise of her flesh. She ran her fingers through his hair, pressing him to her, and felt his tongue travel to the softness of her belly, his cheek against the jut of her pelvis. The sarong slithered to the floor, joining the small heap of his own clothes.

With the inevitability of the sun sinking to join the horizon, he sought out that secret place, where she was at once most vulnerable and most sensitive. Her response leaped like fire through her body. She threw back her head, crying out her pleasure, her body quivering like a bow strung too taut.

And then he was gone from there and she was being lifted to the bed to lie on her back, Troy's big body hovering over her. As she whimpered with need, he said huskily, 'There's time, Lucy. We have all day and all night and nothing but the two of us...'

Far beyond fear or shyness, she wrapped her legs around him and drew him down to lie on top of her, her hips moving under his. He took her breast in his mouth, his hands roaming all her softness and her curves until she thought she would die with the intensity of her desire. Then he was kissing her again, fierce, hard kisses whose demands she was more than ready to meet. She let her palms slide down his spine to circle his hips, and with a gentleness that yet had its own demand, she wrapped her fingers around the very center of his need.

A shudder ran through his body. He gasped her name, his face convulsing as she caressed him. Stilling her hand, he reached for the little envelope he had left by the bed; only then did he thrust down to meet her. She was more than ready. Arching her hips, she took him in, watching the expression chase across his face one after the other: excitement and desire, tenderness and hunger, and the most elemental concentration as the storm gathered within him.

He rolled over on his side, slowing his strokes by an effort of willpower she could only guess at, touching her with a sureness and sensitivity that quickened her breathing until she was panting out loud, her nails digging into his arms. Then he was on top of her again and her body strained to meet his, unable to bear even the most temporary of separations. The tendons were corded in his neck, his breathing tortured in her ears.

Their bodies rocked and surged together, playing with surfaces, only to plunge deeper and deeper into the reefs of passion, where the water was the mysterious blue that blurred boundaries, where the never-ending dance of life and death was played out. The tides seized her, the currents whirled her about, the rhythms of her body inseparable from Troy's, until she lost all control, all sense of who she, Lucy, was. She became him, swam within him to depths that were shot with light, and in a crashing of foam in the black darkness of a cave lost herself and joined with him.

They clung together for what seemed like a very long time to Lucy, although it might have been only a few minutes. The din of her heartbeat gradually subsided; she grew aware of herself, of her body as a separate entity held in the arms of a man called Troy—and felt a pang of loss for a union that had been unlike any she had ever known. Troy's back was slick with sweat. Stroking it, she opened her eyes.

He was gazing at her face as if he had never seen it before, as though something new had been revealed to him that had knocked him off balance. He said hoarsely, 'What just happened... I've never felt like that in my life. I—I lost myself in you, Lucy.'

He suddenly dropped his head to her breast. She tightened her hold, whispering, 'I lost myself and found you.'

'It was like that for you, too?'

'Oh, yes... couldn't you tell?'

As he looked up emotions were chasing each other across his face, and none of them was less than intense. She said fiercely, with no idea where the words came from, 'You're safe with me, Troy. I swear you are.'

He let out a long, jagged breath. 'Deep waters,' he said.

Too deep for me to know where I am... Too deep to see where I'm going. Lucy pushed his hair back from his forehead, feeling where it, too, was damp with sweat, and felt her heart clench with love for him.

He rested his cheek on her breast again. She curved her arms around him, knowing that, although she was sailing through unknown seas without a chart to guide her, she had never felt happier or more complete than she did now, in Troy's bed, with the heavy pounding of his heart against her belly.

The slow minutes passed. Lucy was almost asleep when Troy stirred, murmuring into her throat, 'I'll be back in a minute.'

He went to the bathroom. When he came back, he stood at the foot of the bed looking down at her. She was lying on her back, her mahogany hair a tangle on the pillow, her cheeks still flushed from the act of love.

She raised one knee and gave him a lazy, provocative smile. 'Are you coming back to bed?'

He grinned at her. 'Is the sea blue?' Sitting down beside her, he let his eyes wander over the long lines of her body, so completely exposed to him.

In a low voice Lucy said, 'You don't even have to touch me, and I want you.'

He ran one hand from her ankle up the length of her leg, letting it rest where her thighs joined. 'So doing this has no effect?' he asked innocently.

'Well . . . I wouldn't go that far.'

His fingers moved with exquisite sensitivity. 'How far would you go, dearest Lucy?'

The tenderness in his face was almost more than she could bear. There was more than one way to tell him she loved him, she thought, and said quietly, 'To the land beyond the sea where the sun never sets . . . that far.'

'I believe you would.' Shifting to lie against her, he threw one leg over hers, its weight like an anchor holding her in a safe harbor. Then he kissed her parted lips.

They made love without haste, with a new sureness and a level of trust that both emboldened Lucy and let her expose her vulnerabilities more openly. This time the storm built slowly, although with the same inevitable momentum as before; Troy brought her to the very brink before releasing her along with his own shuddering surrender. Afterward he fell asleep in her arms, as suddenly as a child might, and she curled against the warmth and solidity of the body that was already so well known to her, and wondered, not altogether facetiously, if one could die of joy.

He didn't sleep for long, and when he woke Lucy had indisputable evidence that he was more than interested in her. She said, trailing little kisses across his shoulder,

'To think that when we went for a swim I was afraid you didn't want to make love to me.'

'You now have a choice—barbecued chicken or me.'

'Who's doing the cooking?'

'I am. Are you trying to tell me that chicken breasts take preference over this?' He brushed her nipple suggestively with his palm.

He looked young and carefree and very happy. 'Are you serving salad with the chicken?' she asked, wide-eyed.

His hand moved lower. 'Indeed,' he said.

They came together in laughter; then they got up and shared the shower. Lucy wound the sarong low over her hips; Troy tucked another hibiscus behind her ear. They ate on the deck, watching the last vestige of orange fade from the sky, candles casting a small aura of light in the gathering darkness. Troy and she made easy conversation—he questioning her about her job, her apartment and her friends.

After he had fetched one of his shirts, which he put around her shoulders against the evening's chill, she smiled her thanks and said, 'You know, something's become very clear to me the last couple of weeks. I love my job—it's what I want to do—but I've been going about it all the wrong way, killing myself with busy-ness, working from eight in the morning often to eight at night. One massage after another with no rest in between. Totally counter to the whole spirit of massage... No wonder I got sick.'

He said bluntly, 'Why were you doing that?'

'I've always known my family didn't approve of what I do.' Lucy took another sip of wine, swirling the glass so the flames splintered against the crystal. 'So without ever thinking about it, I ran my job in a way they would approve. Worked from dawn to dusk, paid all my debts, built up a large clientele that's now running me instead of the other way round.' She grimaced. 'Stupid, huh?'

'Understandable, I'd say.'

'When I go back——' she looked down, feeling the full impact of her words '—I'll have to make some changes.'

Troy gripped her wrist with bruising strength. 'This has all happened so fast—too fast. We both have to go back, Lucy. Me to Vancouver, you to Ottawa.'

Where they would be separated by more than two thousand miles. 'I know we do,' she said, rather proud of the steadiness of her voice. And, partly because she was terrified of the abyss that yawned in front of her at the prospect of being separated from Troy, she said, 'I don't want to talk about it now. This is time out—isn't that what you said?'

'I'm not so sure that that particular phrase has any meaning where you and I are concerned.'

Only wanting to banish the grimness from his face, she went on, 'I've also figured out why sailing meant so much to me when I was a kid.'

'The best years of your life...'

She nodded, somehow not surprised that he had remembered. 'My mother and my sisters are all petite, elegant women. At thirteen I towered over them, and over everyone else in my class at school—including all the boys. I felt such a misfit, so out of place in a body that wouldn't stop growing. But when I went sailing, and discovered the magic of wind and water, everything suddenly made sense. Because I was tall, I could hoist sails and hike out with the best of them...so I forgot all about being self-conscious.' She said, with a touch of the old pain, 'It sure beat being a wallflower at school dances.'

With an underlying note of anger Troy asked, 'Did your mother know how you felt?'

'Oh, no, I couldn't have talked to her about it. She was so busy, always working or entertaining or going to concerts... You're the first person I've ever told.'

'You must have felt very lonely.'

'Yes...yes, I did.' Her voice had thinned, for to whom had she ever admitted that before?

'I'm glad you told me,' he said.

As she smiled into Troy's eyes, Lucy found herself wondering if this was yet another dimension of love: sitting up at midnight talking about things that mattered with someone who listened, understood and cared. Because Troy cared, she'd swear he did. With a start she realized something else. Her years of sailing had been the best years of her life because at the stern of a Laser she had become one—body and soul. The same thing had happened this afternoon. Every atom in her body, every fantasy and thought and wish and dream, had merged in her union with Troy, just as Heather Merritt had assured her it would. Body and soul, she was Troy's. And that, too, was what love meant.

She couldn't tell him that. Not yet.

'You've gone a long way away, Lucy.'

She glanced up. 'Sorry,' she muttered. 'This is all new to me—you and I together like this. I suppose I'm frightened.'

'Yeah,' he said, 'I know the feeling.' He looked down at his plate. 'Have you had enough? Do you want coffee?'

She stood up, his shirt falling open to reveal the pale gleam of her breasts. 'Take me to bed, Troy.'

He matched her urgency in the speed with which he pushed back his chair. Pausing only to blow out the candles, so the darkness was absolute, he led her into the house and down the hall to the bedroom. And there all Lucy's thoughts of past or future were lost in the immediacy of the present.

She woke sometime in the night. It was still dark. Through the window she could see the stars hanging low over the islands in the channel. Then Troy made a small, choked sound of pain, as though someone were strangling him, and she realized it must have been that that had wakened her. His fist was clenched on the pillow by her head; his shoulders, even in sleep, were hunched. Moving as carefully as she could, she knelt beside him and began stroking the length of his spine, her touch firm without being intrusive.

When his eyes flew open, she sensed the effort it took for him to adjust to where he was. He pushed himself up on his elbow, rubbing at his face. 'Lucy...was I dreaming?'

'I think you must have been.'

He reached out for her blindly. She sank down into his arms, feeling him pull her close with a desperation that in the last few hours had gone into abeyance. 'Hold on to me,' he rasped. 'Just don't let go... Oh, Lucy, you're so full of life and warmth, I need you so much.'

She clasped him with all her strength, and beneath the happiness that he should need her she was afraid again. 'Deep waters,' Troy had said earlier. Deep waters, indeed. And how was she to fathom them when she had been given less than twenty-four hours?

She stayed awake long after Troy had fallen asleep again, her eyes burning with tiredness, her brain going round and round the little she knew about him. Of facts she had painfully few. But she knew the essentials, she thought stoutly. She knew, because she had made love with him, that he was generous and passionate. She knew he could laugh. And now she knew that he needed her.

It had to be enough. Because it was all she had.

She did eventually go to sleep herself. When she woke in the morning, the bedside clock said nine-thirty and she was alone in the big bed; she could hear Troy showering, singing loudly and rather tunelessly to himself. She hadn't meant to sleep so late. They had so little time here—how could she have wasted it sleeping?

She cleaned her teeth and had a quick shower, then wrapped the sarong around her body and went out on the deck. In the far corner a lizard regarded her un-winkingly. A male lizard, she soon decided, as it per-formed the reptilian equivalent of a push-up and puffed a rather beautiful scarlet and yellow disc from its throat. It seemed content to keep on repeating this performance without any noticeable results. When Troy joined her on the deck, clean-shaven, with a white towel swathed around his hips, she said, 'If I were a lady lizard, I'd call him irresistible.'

Troy watched in amusement. 'Now, why can't I do that?' he said.

'I find what you do entirely adequate.'

'Only adequate, Lucy? I can see I'll have to expand my repertoire.'

He advanced on her, grinning. Sun and shadow pat-terned his deep chest, while the wind from the sea was playing with his thick blond hair. Lucy held her ground, wishing she could freeze time and keep him always with her, infected in spite of herself by the laughter in his face. 'I want breakfast,' she announced.

'You prefer papaya to me? Oh, Lucy...'

With a speed that took her by surprise he whipped his arms around her and lifted her off the ground, tossing her over his shoulder. As she shrieked in mock terror, he headed single-mindedly for the bedroom. Giggling helplessly, pounding with her fists on his back, Lucy gasped, 'Real pirates have beards. And eye patches.'

He flung her down on the bed and threw himself on top of her, pinioning her wrists to the mattress. 'Quit complaining—at least I own a boat.'

'An apprentice pirate.' Her eyes were laughing up at him and the sarong had slipped. The smile wiped from his face, Troy said with sudden harshness, 'You're so beautiful...so unbearably beautiful. Every time we make love, I end up wanting you more than the last time.' Still holding her captive, he began kissing her, impassioned kisses that spoke elementally of possessiveness.

Her arms might be immobile; her hips were not. Lucy thrust against him, and heard him groan her name deep in his throat. And not once, in the next half-hour, did she think about breakfast.

CHAPTER NINE

LUCY and Troy did eat breakfast eventually, croissants that Troy had taken out of *Seawind's* freezer, with fruit and iced coffee decorated with whipped cream. Lucy licked her lips. 'Decadent,' she said contentedly. She did feel content, far more than content; how could she not with Troy as her lover? She was also trying hard to ignore how rapidly the sun was climbing in the sky.

Echoing her thoughts, Troy said, 'Let's have a swim before we head back.'

Twenty-four hours had been just long enough to give her a taste of paradise—how could she leave here? 'All right,' she said.

'I don't want to go, either, Lucy. But we have to.'

'Another should,' she said wryly.

'The next family'll be with us for a week; we'll have lots to do back at the dock.'

'Who are they?'

'The name's deVries. Valerie, Charles and their nineteen-year-old daughter Shannon. They're from Montreal, if I remember rightly.' He drained his coffee. 'I'll clean up the food—why don't you try out the hammock?'

He didn't want her company, was that what he was saying? Or was she being ridiculously over-sensitive? Lucy lay back in the hammock, feeling the soft cotton cord taut against her bare legs, letting the hammock rock back and forth so that the vines and the high clouds dipped and swayed in her vision. Nothing fixed, she thought, nothing firm, and wondered in cold terror if she would ever came back to this enchanted place.

She was being a fool. In the last twenty-four hours Troy and she had been intimate in ways she couldn't have imagined; he wasn't simply going to go away.

Back and forth her thoughts carried her, until she stopped the hammock by placing one foot on the floor. The lizard was watching her from the corner of the deck; her foot braced on the deck, one arm dangling, she craned her neck to keep it in sight, wondering if it would repeat its mating ritual. Staying absolutely still, she waited, feeling the pull of muscles across her belly.

'*Lucy*! My God, Lucy...'

Awkwardly, because she had a crick in her neck, she looked around. Troy was standing in the doorway staring at her. He was ashen-faced, half leaning against the frame as though he needed its support. 'What's wrong?' she cried, lurching to her feet. In a rustle of dead leaves the lizard slithered away through the undergrowth.

His voice scarcely recognizable, Troy said, 'For a moment I—I thought you were dead.'

'*Dead*?'

'The way you were lying, your head all twisted...'

She could have made some flip remark, but he was white about the mouth and she could see the tendons stand out in his wrist where he was gripping the wood. 'I'm fine,' she said prosaically, 'I was watching the lizard.'

He straightened, rubbing his palms down his shorts. 'I seem to have made a fool of myself,' he said levelly. 'Are you ready to swim?'

'I'm sorry I scared you.'

'It was nothing—a trick of the light. Let's go.'

For Troy the subject was closed; he pivoted and disappeared into the house. When Lucy went to put her bikini on he wasn't in the bedroom, and when she went outside on the deck she could see him running headlong into the sea, as if a pack of hounds were baying at his heels. He dove under the waves and surfaced doing a fast, efficient crawl. Alone, she walked down to the beach.

Although the water was deliciously warm and crystal-clear, Lucy knew she didn't want to be there. Troy was still stroking back and forth across the width of the bay without a wasted motion. In spirit as well as in body, she thought, watching him, he'd already left her behind. She lay on her back, floating idly, until he finally waded to shore. Shaking the water from his hair, he said, 'Why don't we shower on *Seawind*? It won't take me a minute to get our gear, and the couple who look after the house will be over later today.'

Lucy didn't want to think of anyone else in the rooms where she had known such happiness. She had meant to keep her feelings to herself but she blurted, 'I don't want to leave.'

As he reached for his towel, which he'd left lying on the sand, and rubbed at his chest, she felt a shaft of desire as piercing as if they'd never once made love in the big bed in his room. He said brusquely, 'You think I want to go? Get real, Lucy. No matter how many times I stay here, I never want to leave.'

She waded the last few feet into shore. 'So it's nothing to do with me—is that what you're saying? It's the place?'

'Are you trying to pick a fight?'

I want you to tell me you love me, she thought, and for a horrible moment was afraid she'd said the words out loud. 'I don't know what I'm doing,' she said, speaking the literal truth. 'We'd better go.'

'You knew before we got here that we only had a day.'

'Stop being so damned rational!'

'Oh, for Pete's sake,' he exclaimed, and marched up the beach toward the house.

Lucy watched him go, her nails digging into her palms. Sex, she thought. She'd been deceiving herself to think that the past few hours had had any significance for Troy other than the physical, that his need of her was anything more than a simple craving for her body. Her elder sister Marcia had always said—in her cool, well-bred voice—that men were like that. 'Trapped by testosterone,' had been Marcia's phrase. She, Lucy, should have paid more attention.

Because Troy hadn't said he loved her. Had never mentioned the word.

And they were back to fighting again.

Lucy discovered that she was shivering. She picked up her own towel and wrapped it around her, and as Troy reappeared went to help him with the dinghy. A few minutes later she was climbing on the transom of *Seawind*. Two weeks ago she couldn't possibly have imagined that she would ever be reluctant to do this.

The boat was exactly as they had left it. It was she who had changed.

She quickly went forward, found her loosest shorts and most unrevealing T-shirt, and got dressed. And as they motored out of the bay she didn't give the villa even one last glance.

Because Troy used the engine all the way back to Road Town, Lucy went below, where she worked out her menus and made a grocery list, cleaning out the refrigerator as she did so. She then stripped all the beds and bundled the laundry together. By the time Troy was ready to anchor *Seawind* at the dock, she had already started cleaning one of the cabins, concentrating grimly on what she was doing.

Jack caught the mooring lines as Troy flung them ashore. 'Message for you,' he said affably, fishing in his back pocket. 'From your next lot of guests.' Maybe they'd cancelled, Lucy thought longingly. 'Think they want to come on board tonight,' Jack added.

Troy unfolded the sheet of paper. 'Their travel agent fouled up the hotel booking,' he grunted. 'As long as they come after dinner I suppose we could be ready— Lucy?'

She and Troy wouldn't even have tonight alone on *Seawind*. 'If that's what you want,' she said crisply.

He shot her an unfriendly glance. 'Gavin makes a point of giving extra service—that's how he's trying to increase his bookings. I don't think we have much choice.'

Jack raised his brows and wandered off, whistling to himself. Lucy said despairingly, 'Troy, I can't stand this.'

Her shoulders had drooped; she looked very unhappy. Troy said flatly, 'It was time to leave the villa, Lucy. You've got to accept that.'

'Don't you have any feelings for me at all?' she cried.

He gave an ugly laugh. 'I sure have . . . I think you've bewitched me.'

She wasn't at all sure she liked that word. 'You look less than ecstatic to be under my spell.'

'I don't know what the devil's happening to me!'

'Sex,' Lucy said, her chin raised defiantly.

He shot her a poisonous glance. 'Is that all it was for you? The twenty-four-hour equivalent of a dirty weekend?'

'That's what it was for you.'

'Don't you tell me what I'm feeling!' he roared.

'The entire dock's going to know what you're feeling!'

'I thought it was men who were always guilty of separating sex from emotion,' he grated. 'Not that we have the time to stand here arguing the subtleties of human sexual behavior. Give me the grocery list and the laundry and I'll go and phone the deVrieses; they left me a contact number.'

'I have more than enough emotion for the two of us,' Lucy pronounced, and stamped down the companionway stairs.

He followed her, shoving the list in his pocket and picking up the bundled sheets and towels. 'Don't fall in love with me, Lucy. I'm warning you.'

'I wouldn't think of it,' said Lucy, and waited until he had gone before allowing herself the luxury of regaling the mahogany walls of the saloon with her entire stock of profanity. Then she started cleaning bathrooms, a task as far removed from romance as it could be.

Troy was in his cabin changing when the deVries family arrived. Lucy, now wearing her favorite purple shorts with a flowered shirt, heard them coming down the dock and went out on deck to meet them. She took to them instantly, for all three were blessed with the twin gifts of warmth and charm.

Charles, it transpired, played the cello in a chamber group that was establishing a solid reputation across the continent; tonsured like a monk, he sported a trim black beard. His wife, Valerie, had haunting dark eyes and a haircut as elegant as her bearing, and their daughter, Shannon, was stunning: dark blue eyes, sleek blonde hair that fell straight down her back, and an astonishing degree of self-assurance for someone her age. She was everything that Lucy wasn't: small and delicate, with a slender, almost boyish figure. Yet somehow this didn't bother Lucy; the stay at Troy's villa, however tempestuously it had ended, had removed any desire to look other than she did.

She welcomed them aboard, and called Troy's name. Then she led them down into the saloon, showing them the cabins. Shannon had just come out of the forward cabin she was going to occupy, and was laughing at something her father had said, when Troy came down the stairs. Lucy saw his eyes fly to the young woman with the sheaf of pale, silken hair. He stopped dead in his tracks, gripping the railing. He looked, Lucy thought blankly, as though someone had just punched him in the stomach. As though he couldn't breathe.

She made a tiny move toward him, for the agony in his eyes was beyond any she had ever seen, but then Charles stepped out of his cabin and said pleasantly, 'You must be our skipper... Charles deVries. My wife, Valerie, and our daughter, Shannon.'

Troy swallowed hard, and with a superhuman effort got himself under control. He let go of the railing and walked across the polished floor to shake hands, and only Lucy would have known that he moved with none of his usual lithe grace. He held Shannon's hand as briefly as politeness would allow, his smile a mere movement of his lips, and said, 'Lucy's planning hot chocolate and cookies on deck whenever you're settled. In the meantime I'll show you how the plumbing works and give you a tour of the boat.'

Lucy, who was so attuned to him, heard the strain under his commonplace words, and knew he hadn't yet recovered from the shock Shannon's appearance had caused him. He must have been in love with a woman who looked like Shannon, she thought sickly. Someone he had never told her about... The same woman who had fueled his rage that night on the beach. How else to explain his reaction?

The memory of Rosamund, to whom he had once been engaged and who had never stirred his emotions, couldn't possibly have dealt such an impact.

Obediently Lucy went to the galley to prepare the hot chocolate, which she served on deck along with fresh coconut cookies she had baked after supper. Valerie leaned back, gazing at the myriad stars. 'A perfectly lovely ending to a dreadful day,' she said. 'We were delayed in Boston, Lucy, and we only just made the flight in San Juan. Then to find there were no vacancies at the hotel... It was very good of you to take us on board this evening.'

'It means we can make an earlier start in the morning,' Lucy rejoined.

'Not too early...I'm on vacation.' At Lucy's look of inquiry Valerie added, 'I normally go to work at seven, I'm a hospital administrator.'

She looked too chic to do anything so mundane. Lucy glanced at Troy to see if he had heard this. But Troy was oblivious to Valerie and Lucy; he was watching Shannon, who was arguing amicably with her father over who should have the last cookie. 'Remember your tuxedo,' Shannon joked.

'I never do up the buttons when I'm playing,' Charles said loftily. 'Sugar's bad for your complexion, you know that.'

Valerie said mildly, 'You could break the cookie in half.'

'Or I could get more from the galley,' Lucy offered. 'And who'd like more hot chocolate?'

Charles, who was clearly a hedonist, pushed his mug across the table. 'Troy?' Lucy asked.

Troy was still staring at Shannon and didn't hear her. This is nothing to do with memory, Lucy thought in terror. This is about here and now. Troy's attracted to

Shannon—moth to her flame. He can't take his eyes off her.

Clumsily she gathered the mugs and fled to the galley, but her thoughts pursued her like sharks after blood. Troy had fallen in love with Shannon. People did fall in love at first sight. They couldn't help it. It was a force of nature, ungovernable, impossible to resist. She herself had done it more than once.

It seemed the cruelest of ironies that Shannon should be blonde.

And how could he have fallen for Shannon only hours after making love with her, Lucy?

She dropped two cookies on the floor, had to sweep up the crumbs, and nearly let the milk boil over on the stove. But eventually she got herself together and went back up on deck. To a casual onlooker the scene could have been one from a tourist brochure: five vacationers relaxing on the deck of a yacht under a star-jeweled southern sky. But to Lucy, so acutely aware of the undercurrents, it was more like a scene from a surreal play. She talked and laughed, she discussed possible sailing routes and extolled the pleasures of snorkeling, and all the while she was watching her facile performance with a distant amazement.

Finally, to her infinite relief, Valerie got to her feet and stretched. 'I'm for bed,' she said.

Charles stood up too, slipping an arm around his wife's waist, and Shannon said with a gamine grin at Troy, 'I'd better get my beauty sleep if I'm going to learn to snorkel tomorrow.' She smiled at Lucy. 'Thanks for the wonderful cookies... See you tomorrow.'

The minute their backs were turned Troy pushed up from the table in an explosion of movement. Before Lucy could say a word, he'd leaped out of the cockpit and was striding forward. Lucy cleared off the table, put the

food away in the galley, washed the dishes and set up
the coffee-machine for the morning. Then she switched
out the lights and went forward herself, stepping round
the open hatches of the deVrieses' cabins.

Her blue duffel bag was sitting by the hatch to Troy's
cabin. With another pang of terror she saw that Troy
was standing waiting for her at the bow, holding on to
the headstay. He said, so quietly that she had to strain
to hear him, 'I've got to be alone tonight, Lucy—I'm
sorry.'

The worst thing was that Lucy wasn't really surprised;
unconsciously she had been expecting something like this.
She stepped closer, aching to touch him yet afraid to do
so. 'Please, Troy... Just tell me what's going on.'

As if the words choked him, he said, 'I can't.'

She made one more try. 'Were you in love with
someone who looked like Shannon...someone who
died?'

'Leave it, Lucy. Just leave it, will you?'

'Don't shut me out!'

It was a cry of pain. He seized her by the arm and
whispered furiously, 'We aren't going to have a fight
within earshot of our guests—do you hear?'

She said bitterly, 'That's why you were waiting up here
rather than in the cabin. So we couldn't quarrel.' She
looked down, the sight of his long fingers on her flesh
filling her with an agony of loss. He must have fallen
in love with Shannon; it was the only way she could explain his behavior. Blindly she struck out at him.

He dropped her arm, and over the soft lapping of the
water she heard his tormented breathing. Knowing she
was going to weep, and far too proud to do so in front
of him, she picked up her bag and steadily walked aft.
She went down the stairs and into the stern cabin, closing
the door.

Leaning against its smooth mahogany panels, she discovered with dull wonder that now she was alone she couldn't cry. Her throat was too tight, her misery too abject for tears. All her movements jerky and uncoordinated, she put her bag down, unzippered it and pulled out the nightgown that she had never worn in Troy's bed.

And not even that made her cry.

The next five days were the nearest Lucy could imagine to purgatory. It was the falsity of everything she did that was the most difficult to bear. On the surface everything was going smoothly. She cooked some excellent meals and kept the saloon and galley spotless. She crewed for Troy with an efficiency that perhaps only he would have seen as mechanical. She snorkeled with the deVries at the cluster of rocks called the Indians, guided them around the shops in Spanish Town, and led them through the huge tumbled boulders at the southern end of Virgin Gorda. The whole family was having a good time; Lucy had a dim sense of satisfaction that this should be so.

But underneath all this her heart felt as though it were congealing, turning slowly to ice in her breast. She had heard often enough that hearts broke. A clean event— sharp and painful in the moment, and then over and done with—that was how she had pictured it. But for her there was no clean break, only the protracted agony of being constantly in the presence of the man who had once been her lover. For Troy, whom she loved, had turned into a hard-eyed stranger.

There were times she thought she'd dreamed the twenty-four hours at his villa, that they were a figment of her imagination, an elaborate fantasy fed by the lush beauty of the islands and the heat of the sun. There were times she even wondered if she was going out of her mind. What she had believed to be real, more real than anything that had ever happened to her—Troy's arms around her, his body covering her, his kisses inflaming her—had vanished utterly. In place of that reality was another: a tall, blond man whom she couldn't reach. Who had turned his back to her with a profound finality.

It was a repeat of the old pattern, a pattern she had thought was gone forever.

Images stood out from those five days. The ugly spasm that had thinned Troy's mouth when Shannon rested a hand on his shoulder as she had jumped down into the dinghy. The tension in his big body when she had accidentally collided with him on the companionway stairs. The way her laughter always riveted him to the spot, his hands stopping whatever task he had been doing.

Once, only a few days ago, Lucy might have expected him to react to her this way. But not any longer.

Not that Troy was seeking Shannon out. If anything, he was avoiding her. He didn't flirt with her. He rarely spoke to her unless she spoke first. But Lucy could tell that he was always aware of her, tied to her by an invisible cord that was stronger than the lines on *Seawind*, and it was this that turned her heart to ice.

On the sixth morning Lucy took Charles, Valerie and Shannon to the boutiques at Soper's Hole, at the western tip of Tortola. Troy had anchored at the most distant mooring so she steered the dinghy between the yachts toward the wooden dock. Everyone got out. Lucy knew it was Valerie's birthday later in the week, and wasn't surprised when Shannon took her father's arm and said brightly, 'You go that way, Mum, we'll meet up with you in half an hour at the bar.'

Valerie smiled as the two of them marched away. 'Shannon has yet to learn the subtle approach... Lucy, why don't you go back to *Seawind*? We'll be at least an hour, it always takes Charles ages to make his mind up... and you look tired,' she finished delicately.

Lucy flushed, knowing Valerie was far too discreet to allude directly to the tension between Lucy and Troy, and far too intelligent to be unaware of it. 'Troy's expecting me to stay here,' she said lamely.

'It's never good to be too predictable,' Valerie remarked, watching the palm fronds curve in the wind.

Why shouldn't she go back to *Seawind*? thought Lucy. She had nothing whatever to lose, and if all she gained was a rip-roaring fight she might at least feel better afterward. 'Whenever you're ready to come back to the boat, sit on one of the benches by the bar and I'll come and get you,' she said, adding awkwardly, 'Thank you, Valerie.'

'I'm sure you're old enough to know that things aren't always what they seem,' Valerie said with characteristic obliqueness. 'Now, I'd better pick up some souvenirs for my nephews.'

She wandered off, her silk skirt blowing against her slender legs. Lucy got back in the dinghy and pulled the starter cord quickly before she could lose her nerve. She cut the engine before she reached *Seawind*, pleased to see that two other dinghies were circling the area. She wasn't sure why she wanted to catch Troy off-guard; perhaps because she had so few other weapons at her command.

But as she tied the dinghy's painter to the transom, she heard music coming form the tape deck in the saloon. Troy had never evinced any interest in the collection of tapes in the drawer of the chart desk, she realized, frowning slightly in puzzlement. The music was beautiful, a solo flute producing ripples and cascades of sound, joyous and unrestrained: a performance entailing a formidable level of technical ability.

She climbed out of the dinghy and stood still for a minute, letting the melody weave its spell, feeling something akin to peace for the first time in many days. Maybe it was a good sign that Troy was listening to such exquisite music; she might finally be able to reach him.

She slipped off her canvas shoes and walked toward the hatch, her bare feet soundless. But as she descended the first of the steps into the saloon she came to a halt. Troy was sitting in one of the swivel chairs. His head was buried in his hands, his back a long curve of abject defeat.

She acted without thought. 'Troy...' she said, and took the rest of the stairs in a rush.

His head jerked up; his cheeks, Lucy saw, were streaked with tears. She stretched out her hand in compassion, but before she could say anything the bleakness in his slate-gray eyes was replaced by a fury that was instant and all-encompassing. He surged to his feet. 'Get out!'

'But——'

He advanced on her in two swift steps. 'Didn't you hear me? Get the hell out of here!'

Every instinct in her body was impelling her to run. But a vestige of courage—or perhaps mere stubbornness—kept Lucy glued to the floor. 'What's the *matter*?' she cried. 'I can't stand being left in the dark— if you've fallen in love with Shannon at least have the decency—and the guts—to tell me so.'

For a moment the torment in Troy's face was replaced by sheer incredulity. 'In love with Shannon? Of course I'm not.'

'Then what's going *on*?'

'I'll tell you what's going on,' he said viciously. 'You've intruded on the first five minutes of privacy I've had in weeks.'

Her nails digging into her palms, Lucy said, 'When you made love to me, you told me you needed me.'

'I sure don't need you poking and prying into my affairs!'

'What are you afraid of?' she flared. 'Showing an emotion—any emotion—that's not anger? Is that what you're afraid of?'

He took a single step toward her, his fists bunched at his sides. 'Let me tell you something, Lucy. I'm entitled to my anger. I'm——'

'*Why*?' she demanded, and with a detached part of her brain heard the flute caress a series of notes as limpid as moonlight on water.

Deep lines scoring his cheeks, Troy said, 'I'll tell you why. And maybe that'll get you off my back. You hear that music? That's my kid sister playing. Lydia. She was studying music in New York, they predicted a brilliant future for her, and one evening last October she walked into her local corner store to buy a loaf of bread and was shot point-blank by the man who'd just robbed the till. They never caught him. She died instantly.'

The flute slipped effortlessly into a plaintive minor key and Lucy whispered, 'She looked like Shannon.'

'Clever girl,' Troy sneered. 'The man who fired that gun—I could kill him with my bare hands. How's that for an expression of emotion?'

Flawless and gloriously beautiful, the melody wove through his words. 'I'm so sorry,' Lucy said, and reached out one hand, her fingers lightly trembling.

'Don't touch me!' he grated. 'He killed her as easily as this——' In a gesture shocking in its violence he hit the stop button on the tape deck. With an ugly metallic click the music ceased as if it had never been.

Into the silence Lucy said, 'Have you ever cried for her, Troy? Sat down and wept your heart out because she's dead?'

Spacing each word as if it were a bullet, he said, 'Get out of here—now.'

Her cheeks as white as *Seawind's* sails, Lucy stayed where she was. 'You've got to grieve for her,' she said, the words tumbling one over the other. 'I was too young to grieve for my father so I carried him like an albatross for years. The woman who played that music—she must have been wondrously alive. She deserves your tears. Because otherwise you're choosing death, you're——'

'Are you quite finished?' Troy rasped. 'Because if you are, you can go up those steps and out of my sight—I can't stand being in the same room with you.'

He meant it. Meant every word. A hard lump clogging her throat, Lucy groped behind her for the galley countertop and backed away from him. He'd said to her once that he was unreachable and intended to remain so; he'd meant that, too. Her ankle struck the lowest of the companionway steps. Turning, Lucy bolted up them.

She tripped on the third step, barking her shins and grabbing at the hatch for support. At the top she whirled to face Troy. 'I hate you,' she said in a choked voice. 'I wish I'd never met you.' Then she ran for the dinghy, where sunlight sparkled on water whose vibrant blues and greens were the antithesis of violent death.

The dinghy started at the first tug on the cord. Lucy hauled in the painter and headed for the opposite shore, away from the boats and the marina. Turning off the motor, she let herself drift with the wind. Her hands gradually stopped shaking; her heart-rate returned to normal. But her ears echoed with the lambent strains of a flute played by a young woman struck down in a senseless act of violence. And in her brain, as inexorable as the ticking of a clock, the same words sounded and resounded: it's over, it's over, it's over...

She and Troy were finished. When they went back to Road Town tomorrow with the deVrieses, she'd quit. Troy could find someone else to cook and crew for him. She, Lucy, was going home.

Because he was never going to change. And she wouldn't beg. There was no point.

She looked around, suddenly loathing the picture postcard prettiness of the moored yachts and the quaint boutiques, not caring if she ever saw another palm tree in her life. She wanted the ordinary streets of home, the meandering Rideau Canal and the wide sweep of the St Lawrence River. She wanted her job and her friends and her family.

She'd never fall in love again. Never. It hurt too much.

Glancing at her watch, she saw that only forty minutes had passed since she'd left Valerie at the dock. She might as well head that way to pick her up.

Once there, Lucy sat down on one of the benches by the bar and ordered a lemonade. She felt blessedly numb inside; maybe her heart had finally frozen solid and was beyond feeling. With any luck at all it would stay that way.

Once she got away from Troy and didn't have to face him every minute of the day, she'd forget him. She'd forget the tragedy that had scarred him so deeply. She'd forget his corrosive rage, his dammed-up grief, his inability to let go of either one. She'd have to.

The lemonade had that reassuring blend of tartness and sweetness that Lucy remembered from childhood. As she was sipping it, Valerie sauntered over to her bench and sat down, showing her the gifts she had bought and describing a painting she was tempted to buy. Not by so much as a glance did she evince any curiosity about what had transpired on *Seawind*. Shannon and Charles arrived ten minutes later, laden with shopping bags and looking very pleased with themselves. 'All set?' Shannon said breezily.

A few minutes later, with immense reluctance, Lucy was following Shannon into the cockpit. But she needn't have worried. Troy didn't even look at her. Automatically she obeyed his soft-spoken commands as they sailed east into the wind, making good speed along the coast. They anchored off Peter Island for lunch.

Lucy was serving ice-cream and strawberries for dessert when Troy came up on deck. Until he spoke, she had had no premonition that the look of gravity on his face was anything to do with her. 'There's a phone call for you, Lucy,' he said in a neutral voice. 'It's your mother.'

The color drained from Lucy's face. Her mother would only call if something was wrong. The memory of Lydia's death flooding her mind, she looked down at the bowl of strawberries, wondering what to do with it, wondering if she was about to hear terrible news again, this time closer to home. As Valerie took the bowl out of her hands, Lucy managed to say, 'I'd better see what she wants,' and hurried below.

The connection was poor, their words booming as if trapped in a cave, but the gist of her mother's message was simple. Lucy's younger sister Catherine had been in a car accident. She was out of intensive care, but still in a serious condition.

'I'm sure she's going to be all right,' her mother said, 'but I—I'd really like to see you.' Even through the crackle of static Lucy could tell that her mother's voice, normally so perfectly controlled, was shaking. 'It's a lot to ask, I know, when you're on holiday, and if you'd rather not, I'd understand. You see, I need you, Lucy... It's funny, Marcia's been wonderful, naturally, but I don't dare cry in front of Marcia—you know how she feels about weepy women. *You* wouldn't mind if I cried, would you, Lucy?'

Catherine wasn't dead. Not like Lydia.

Somehow Lucy found her voice. 'No, Mum, I wouldn't mind. Of course I'll come. Just as soon as I can get a flight... Why don't I call you back in half an hour, once I know what's going on—will you be home?'

'Yes, I'll be here.' There was a pause. 'Thank you, Lucy.'

'I love you, Mum. Half an hour.'

Lucy hung up the phone, her thoughts in chaos. Competent, law-abiding Catherine had failed to slow at a yield sign. She drove a red sports car. Lucy had always liked that car, but today it had failed to protect her sister when another car had collided with it. Catherine could so easily have been killed... Her head spinning, Lucy groped for the nearest chair.

Someone was helping her, a hand guiding her to the chair. She looked down and saw a dusting of blond hair on the back of the hand and in a small, telling gesture thrust it from her. She couldn't bear Troy to touch her. She'd fall to pieces if he did.

Her mother, her cool, detached mother, needed her. Needed her because Lucy was the emotional one in the family, the one who wasn't afraid of tears.

From a long way away she became aware that Troy was speaking to her. 'What's wrong, Lucy? Tell me what's wrong.'

The concern in his face gave her a fleeting glimpse of the old Troy. Feeling her self-control slip another notch, she relayed her mother's message in a flat voice and saw him flinch. 'You'll have to go,' he said. 'I'll radio the airport. I know the people on the desk—we'll get you out on the first flight.'

No ifs or buts; Troy had understood immediately her need to be with her family. Lucy said faintly, 'Who'll cook for you?'

'I'll get in touch with Lise—the woman who used to cook for Gavin. I expect her son's back from San Juan by now.'

Within ten minutes Troy had her a seat on the afternoon flight out of Tortola and tentative bookings all the way to Ottawa, and Lucy had phoned home. When her mother heard she was coming she started to cry, the harsh sobs of someone not used to tears; Lucy's lip was trembling when she put the receiver back and she carefully avoided Troy's eyes.

'We'll head straight for Road Town, it's quicker for you to get to the airport by cab,' he said briefly. 'Let's go.'

Action was what Lucy needed. She hauled in the anchor, and as Troy put the diesel to full power she went to her cabin and packed. It felt strange to put on her skirt with its tidy little roses; it would be cold in Ottawa, she knew.

She was getting her wish. She was going home.

Biting her lip so hard that it bled, she pushed away the nightmare vision of a life without Troy and took one last look round the cabin to make sure she hadn't forgotten anything. Then she went into the galley and organized the evening meal as completely as she could. By then they were coming into Road Harbor. For the last time Lucy reeled out the anchor chain, obeying Troy's hand signals with a stony calm. She said goodbye to the deVrieses, suffering Valerie and Shannon to hug her and Charles to kiss her cheek, then Troy had picked up her bag and they were running along the dock.

'You'll only just make the flight,' he said. 'There's the cab I ordered—I'll tell him he'll have to hurry.' He scrabbled in the pocket of his shorts and pulled out a crumpled piece of paper and a stub of pencil. 'Write down your address and phone number.'

She took the paper, watching him run ahead to the window of the cab. Leaning on her wallet, she wrote in cramped letters, 'I can't bear your anger, Troy—it's better we don't stay in touch.' Then she folded the paper so her message was hidden. When she reached the taxi, she pushed the paper back in his pocket, inwardly shrinking from the contact, and watched him throw her bag in the back seat. She said, not looking at him, 'Thanks for arranging all this, Troy,' and tried to scramble in the cab.

He took her by one shoulder, pulling her round to face him, and said in a savage undertone, 'I know you haven't understood what's been going on. I was a fool not to have——'

'I'll be late,' she cried frantically. 'Let go!'

'I'll see you in Ottawa just as soon as I can get clear of *Seawind*.'

Lucy was doing her best to tug free, her face pale and pinched; it wasn't clear that she had heard him. He kissed her on the mouth with desperate urgency, branding himself on her flesh despite her struggles. 'You know how to reach the boat—let me know how your sister is... I'll see you soon, Lucy.'

No, you won't. You'll never see me again.

She dived into the back seat of the taxi and slammed the door. To her infinite relief the driver, who had a sense for melodrama, took off in a screech of tires. Clenching her hands in her lap, she did not once look back.

It's over, it's over, it's over...

CHAPTER TEN

AT TEN-FORTY-FIVE that night Lucy was ringing her mother's doorbell. She was dazed with tiredness, shivering in the raw night air. The brass knocker and mail slot, set neatly in a fashionably dark blue door, shone with cleanliness; as she remembered the lamps she had polished on *Seawind*, the gnawing pain that had accompanied her every mile of her journey surged up into her throat. Then the door swung open.

'Lucy,' Evelyn Barnes cried, threw her arms around her daughter and dissolved into tears. Lucy, taking the path of least resistance, started to cry too.

Evelyn was the first to pull back. 'Darling,' she quavered, 'you look terrible, and here I am keeping you out on the doorstep.' She pulled Lucy inside and closed the door. 'You'd better have a hot bath and then I'll make you some cocoa.'

'I'm the one who's supposed to be looking after you... Oh, Mum, it's so good to be home! How's Catherine?'

'Better. They've upgraded her condition from serious to stable. She has a broken pelvis and a cracked vertebra, so she'll be there a while. I told her you'd be in to see her in the morning. Now, upstairs with you, Lucy, and we'll talk in a few minutes.'

Lucy grinned. 'Yes, Doctor.'

Evelyn gave her a watery smile in return. 'I behaved so unprofessionally at the hospital this morning—I yelled at the surgeon because I didn't think he was paying enough attention to her symptoms.'

'Truly, Mum? I'd have loved to be there.'

'I'm very glad you weren't. Off you go.'

It was comforting to be told what to do. Lucy's old room at the top of the stairs still had her collection of blue teddy bears lined up on the shelf; the navy-flowered wallpaper and worn Persian rug welcomed her like old friends. She soaked in the hottest water she could bear and put on a fleecy nightgown with a woollen housecoat that she hadn't worn for years and went downstairs. Her mother had lit the fire in the den, where deep green curtains kept out the night. Sinking into her favorite wing chair, Lucy said, 'I feel human again. And you made cranberry muffins—you're an angel.'

Evelyn Barnes was wearing an elegant black caftan made of raw silk, her greying hair pulled back in its usual sleek chignon, her severe features, handsome rather than beautiful, unadorned by make-up. She tucked her tiny feet under her and said in a rush, 'I don't deserve this visit, Lucy—don't think I'm not aware of that.'

Lucy leaned forward, patting her mother on the knee. 'Sure you do.'

'No...' Her mother gazed into the flames. 'Catherine's accident was so sudden and so terrifying, an irrevocable change between one moment and the next. No going back. No re-establishing of the normal. Marcia was wonderful; she took charge of everything. But she was like a machine, and after I'd yelled at the surgeon she read me a little lecture about how medicine is a science and how mothers shouldn't be overly emotional. That's when it hit me—what a disservice I've done you. I know you've always been the odd one out in our family. What I realized today is that you're the only one who's in touch with her feelings. The only one of the four of us. And we made you an outcast because of it.'

With a depth of bitterness that shocked her, Lucy wondered what good it had done her in the past three weeks to be in touch with her feelings. Troy hadn't wanted them, and he had kept his own well-hidden from her. She said, 'Physically and mentally I didn't fit in either, though. Too tall and not clever enough.'

'You were clever in a different way,' Evelyn said drily, 'that we weren't clever enough to value.' She took a big gulp of the red wine she had poured herself and drew herself up a little taller in her chair. 'I even know how it happened. I've never talked to you very much about your father—I'm sorry about that, too. I loved him deeply. He was like you, full of feeling...I suppose that's why I married him. When he died, I buried that side of myself along with him and I never allowed it out again. Not even with my children.'

'Until tonight,' Lucy said gently. So her most vivid memory of her father was to be trusted: a big blond man, laughing, spontaneous, and very much alive.

'I was afraid if you didn't come until tomorrow—or next week—I'd lose the courage to tell you all this.' Evelyn looked right at her daughter. 'I knew how much I needed you today. You don't know how grateful I am that you came right away.'

A tear was coursing down her mother's cheek. Her mother, who never cried. Lucy fell on her knees by Evelyn's chair and hugged her. 'I'm so glad you did tell me.'

They sat up late that night, and as they talked the big blond man who had been Lucy's father became a real person rather than a shadowy figure from her past. When they finally turned out the lights and went upstairs, Lucy tumbled into bed and fell asleep instantly. But when she woke the next morning her first thought was of Troy.

Seawind would have left Road Town, was perhaps anchored in some quiet cove where many-hued fish swam among the coral. Another woman would have taken her place in the galley. And Shannon would still be on board, that beautiful young woman who reminded Troy of his dead sister.

Lucy burrowed under the covers, her body clamoring for Troy's touch, her soul aching for his presence, her mind despising herself for wanting someone who had so decisively turned his back on her. She would never see him again; the note she had written him would make sure of that. She had done the right thing, the only thing in the circumstances. She just wished it didn't hurt so much.

Lucy went to see Catherine as soon as visiting hours permitted. Although Catherine was well enough to be complaining about the public ward she was in, Lucy was shocked by her sister's pallor, by the complicated contraption that held her in traction and by the cuts and scrapes and bruises that marred the austere perfection of Catherine's features. She didn't stay long; Catherine also tired easily.

As she was going down the steps outside, buttoning her raincoat against a wind whose bite felt like winter, a woman's voice hailed her. Marcia, her elder sister, was tapping smartly across the parking lot. Marcia always looked as though whatever she was doing was essential to the smooth running of the world. Lucy offered her cheek to be brushed by her sister's lips. No hugs from Marcia. Marcia didn't like to be touched.

'How's Catherine?' Marcia asked.

As Lucy was describing how she had found her sister, Marcia broke in, 'She's young enough that her bones will knit just fine... I don't understand why Mother's making such a fuss—she's really been impossible since the accident.'

Lucy had forgotten that Marcia rarely listened to the answers to the questions she asked. 'Mum was upset,' she said temperately.

'She's a doctor; she should know better. You look very tanned, Lucy—I hope you're aware of the dangers of UV. By the way, some man left a message for you with my secretary. I can't imagine why you gave him my number.'

Lucy's heart gave a great thump in her chest. 'Who?' she gasped.

With aggravating slowness Marcia searched through the papers in her neat leather purse, eventually extracting a bright pink slip. 'Troy Donovan,' she read. 'He left a number for you to call. I really would prefer that your personal life not overflow into my office.'

'I didn't give him your number. I didn't give him anybody's number,' Lucy said, crumpling the piece of pink paper into a tight ball. 'I'm through with him.'

'I'll have my secretary block his calls, then,' Marcia said briskly, glancing at her gold watch. 'I've only got five minutes to spare with Catherine before I have to be back at work. Nice seeing you, Lucy.'

Lucy clumped down the steps. She had recognized *Seawind's* code numbers right away. But she wasn't going to phone Troy. Not today. Not ever.

When she got home, there was a message from Evelyn's secretary that she was to call Troy Donovan. And when Lucy went to her own office, to pick up her mail and check her answering machine, the very last of a long string of messages made her heart plummet in her chest. To hear Troy's voice—deep, sure of itself, so well-remembered—drained the strength from her knees, so that she sank down on the corner of her desk.

'Lucy,' he said over the hiss of static, 'I can't talk now—privacy and charters don't mix. Would you call me this afternoon and let me know you got home safely and how your sister is?' He then repeated *Seawind's* code and rang off.

She felt the first slow burn of anger and welcomed it with all her heart. Now that she was gone Troy suddenly wanted to talk to her. Too bad, she thought. You had your chance and you didn't take it. You're too late now. She then went back to the beginning of the tape, copied the other messages and erased them all. Thank goodness all four members of the family had unlisted numbers. At least he wouldn't be able to reach her at home.

Anger buoyed her up until bedtime, when more basic appetites vanquished it. Sex is the only issue here, she thought, pounding her pillow into a shape that would encourage sleep. It's nothing to do with love. I don't love Troy anymore, I don't—because if I do, I'm the worst kind of fool.

She was awake until three in the morning, then fell into a deep sleep from which she was awakened by the telephone that stood on the cherrywood desk in the hall. Staggering across the carpet, she picked the receiver up and croaked, 'Hello?'

'Did I wake you, darling?' Evelyn said. 'I'm so sorry, I thought you'd be up by now. Lucy, I've had the oddest phone call from a man called Troy Donovan... He wanted a number where he could reach you, but I thought I should check with you first. He sounded very persuasive, I must say. A gorgeous voice. He even got past Margaret.'

Margaret was Evelyn's secretary, a redoubtable woman. 'You're not to give it to him, Mum! I don't want to talk to him.'

'Is he the reason you look so unhappy?'

Lucy made a face into the telephone; she had thought she'd done a good job at disguising just how unhappy she was. 'That's irrelevant. You can tell him I never want to hear from him again.'

'I think you should be the one to tell him that.'

'Get Margaret to do it,' Lucy said irritably. 'That'll get his attention. I've got to go, Mum, I want to spend some time at the office and start letting my clients know I'm home. Bye.'

Damn him, she fumed, banging the receiver back in its cradle. Couldn't he take a hint? And quelled a traitorous urge to laugh that Troy had charmed his way past Margaret.

She didn't laugh at all when she pressed the message button on her answering machine at the studio. 'I'm coming up to Ottawa as soon as I can, and I'll find you if I have to ransack every goddamned massage outfit in the city,' Troy announced. 'I'll get down on my knees and apologize for being a total idiot, I'll smother you in roses, I'll throw you over my shoulder and haul you to the nearest bed—whatever it takes. But I'm going to see you, Lucy. I have to. Because I love you.'

As abruptly as he had begun, Troy broke the connection. The next message started—someone looking for an appointment. Lucy rewound the tape and listened again, and again Troy ended with the same three words. I love you.

He didn't mean it. How could he? It was lust he felt for Lucy, not love. Lust and rage and repudiation.

Emotions as highly colored as the flowers at Troy's villa tumbled and tossed within her. Lucy got to her feet, looking around as though she wasn't quite sure where she was, all her good intentions about getting to work evaporating. She craved action, anything to take her mind off a man whose next move she didn't even want to contemplate. Catherine. She'd go and see Catherine.

But when she got to the hospital Catherine was less than delighted to see her. A huge florist's box was lying beside her on the bed, the lid tossed to one side. The box was brimming with the most glorious red roses Lucy had ever seen; Catherine was frowning at the card.

As soon as she saw Lucy she demanded, 'Who's this man called Troy? I thought these roses were for me— I'm the one who's ill, after all—but they're for you. Really, Lucy, you might have a little more discretion than to conduct your affairs via my hospital bed.'

Marcia had said something to the same effect.

A rapt silence had fallen over the ward. Lucy blushed as red as the roses and snatched the card from her sister's fingers.

Dearest Lucy,
Red roses are a terrible cliché, I know. But I couldn't get hibiscus, and they do bring all my love.
Troy.

How dared he? How *dared* he? Lucy ripped the card in two and flung the pieces on the floor. 'As far as I'm concerned you can have every one of those roses,' she said, and burst into tears.

The old lady in the next bed, who had spent an enjoyable half-hour the evening before telling Lucy every detail of her hernia operation, sucked in her breath in a gratified sigh.

Catherine snapped, '*Lucy*! You and Mother between you are altogether too much.'

Lucy ripped a handful of tissues from the box by Catherine's bed and noisily blew her nose. 'I hate him,' she snuffled. 'I never want to see him again.'

'So why are you crying?' her sister asked with impeccable logic.

'Oh, Catherine, do shut up!'

'That's scarcely the way to speak to me when I'm so ill,' Catherine said haughtily.

She was right; it wasn't. Lucy scowled, her brain belatedly going into action. 'You know what these horrible roses mean? He's tracked you down. If he comes to Ottawa, this is the first place he'll look for me. He can't go to any of our homes because our phone numbers are unlisted. So he'll come here. What on earth am I going to do?'

'You're in love with him,' Catherine said distastefully, rather as if her sister were suffering from some unmentionable disease.

'Oh, Cat, I don't know.' The childish nickname slipped out before Lucy thought. 'I don't know anything anymore. I feel like I'm under siege, because every time I turn around he's phoning me, and I'm so unhappy I could die, and I'm so angry with him I could kill him, and of course I'm in love with him. Why else would I be making a fool of myself in front of a whole roomful of people?' With defiant panache she blew her nose again.

Catherine relented enough to smile. 'I'm glad I don't make a practice of falling in love if this is what it does to you.'

'He's the skipper of the boat I was on, he's handsome and sexy and he managed to sweet-talk his way past Margaret.'

Catherine's eyes widened with respect. 'He *did*?'

In sudden trepidation Lucy said, 'Cat, you've got to promise you won't tell him where my apartment is.'

In a ritual straight from their childhood, Catherine crossed her hands over her hospital johnny shirt and looked piously up at the ceiling. 'I swear.'

'You're a sweetheart. And now I'm going to take these roses and put them in the chapel downstairs,' Lucy said, jamming the lid on the box with scant respect for the contents, then tucking it under her arm. 'Somebody might as well enjoy them.' She kissed her sister on the cheek. 'Look after yourself... I'll scoot in to see you later today. And remember what you promised.'

The roses looked quite magnificent against the dark-stained woodwork in the chapel; with a pang of compunction Lucy turned her back on them and went outside. It was raining again and there wasn't a leaf to be seen on the trees. Forcing herself into action, she went back to her mother's—she couldn't quite bring herself to face her own apartment yet—and started on the long list of phone calls she had to make.

The next morning, after a night whose dreams would never have made it past the censor board, she went to her office, gave two massages and made a depressingly large hole in her bank account by paying all her bills. Since the delivery of the roses Troy had made no further attempts to get in touch with her. No more phone calls for Margaret, no more talk of love on Lucy's answering machine. Good, thought Lucy, he finally got the message; and tamped down the cold terror that was lurking in her belly as many-armed as an octopus in an underwater cave.

At five past twelve she decided to walk to her mother's for lunch. The house would be empty; she could relax for an hour before paying a quick visit to Catherine and then coming back to work. For the first time since she had arrived, the sun was shining. A pale sun with no noticeable warmth, she thought critically, and could almost feel beneath her sensible city shoes the burning sand on the beach at Troy's villa. The palms would be rustling in the wind, the hibiscus blooms drinking in the sunlight... She pushed open the wrought-iron gate to her mother's front garden and saw the man sitting on the front step.

Her hand froze on the latch. She was dreaming again, calling him up from a need too desperate to be acknowledged. Then Troy stood up and started walking down the path toward her.

He was far too solid-looking to be the figure in a dream. He was unshaven, his eyes dark-circled with tiredness; a leather jacket was slung round his shoulders, over a rumpled shirt and belted trousers. His hair, as usual, was untidy.

Lucy warded him off with a tiny gesture of panic. 'How did you find me here?'

'Catherine gave me the address.'

'She promised she wouldn't!'

'She promised not to give me the address of your apartment... She seems to think you're in love with me.'

'She'll be in more than traction by the time I'm finished with her,' Lucy said vengefully. 'Sure I'm in love with you—that's why I put those awful roses in the hospital chapel and why I haven't answered a single one of your phone calls. You'd better be careful—I'll charge you with harassment.'

He stepped closer. 'Lucy, I——'

'Don't touch me!' she cried. 'I don't know what the *hell* you're doing here but I don't want to talk to you. I don't want to see you ever again. You wouldn't even *talk* to me about your sister. I meant every word of that note I wrote to you in Road Town. I grew up in a family that never spoke of feelings and I don't want anything to do with a man who can't—or won't—share his.'

She seemed to have run out of words. Troy said evenly, 'I was a fool not to tell you about Lydia. But I was afraid if I did that I'd break down in front of Heather or Leona or Shannon—I couldn't handle that. Men aren't supposed to cry—my dad drummed that into me when I was only a kid.'

'Heather and Leona and Shannon weren't at your villa. Only us.'

'I wanted that twenty-four hours to be for you!' he said violently. 'You alone. I loved my sister dearly but I didn't want her intruding on those precious few hours you and I had together.'

A starling chittered from the telephone wire and a truck roared past in a haze of exhaust. 'Lydia comes along with you, Troy,' Lucy said. 'Part of the package.'

'I know that now. But I didn't then—for someone who can put a dozen letters after his name, I've been incredibly stupid.' He looked around unseeingly. 'Can we go inside?'

And Lucy, who had meant never to let him near her again, walked past him and up the steps, unlocked the dark blue door and ushered him indoors. After he had put his bag down on the polished oak floor, she led him into the den. The familiar surroundings steadied her, so that with new discernment she saw the deep lines of tension around his mouth, the exhaustion pulling at his shoulders. 'Would you like something to eat?' she asked.

He shook his head. Standing by her favorite wing chair, he said hoarsely, 'I've got to make you understand... Because if I don't, I've lost you. Don't think I don't know that.' He shrugged out of his jacket, letting it fall on the chair. 'Just tell me one thing, Lucy... Do you love me? Was Catherine right?'

Bracing her back against the other chair, knowing this was a time not for anger but for truth, Lucy said, 'Yes,

I love you. But I won't be with you, Troy, unless you learn not to shut me out. It hurts too much when you do that...you've got to share your feelings.'

Insensibly the lines of his body relaxed. 'I love you, too,' he said. 'More than I can say.'

The dull, grinding ache that Lucy had carried with her ever since she had left his house by the beach began to loosen its hold. Feeling the shift in nerve and muscle, she was nevertheless deeply grateful that Troy made no move to touch her; intuitively he seemed to understand that there were things to be said before their bodies came together. 'Tell me why you were so unreachable,' she said.

He picked up a Venetian paperweight from the coffee-table and turned it over and over in his long fingers. 'Lydia's death nearly killed my mother and father. A murdered child—what parent can cope with that? So I've spent all my free time in the last few months, when I wasn't in the wards or the operating room, trying to hold Mum and Dad together... That's why I didn't get to the villa in February as I usually do. I wanted them to go with me, but they couldn't—it was one of Lydia's favorite places.'

Even in the midst of a compassion stronger than any she had ever felt, a great deal was coming clear to Lucy. 'The one person you didn't look after was yourself,' she said.

'Yeah...my parents came first, my patients second. Even there I wasn't managing very well. I didn't have the energy to care and to listen the way I had always used to, and then I'd feel guilty that I wasn't giving them the best that was in me.'

'You're only human, Troy!'

'When I met you, the timing couldn't have been worse. I'd been chained to Lydia's death for six months. I knew

I had to do something about it, but I didn't have a clue what... and then you applied for the job on *Seawind*.' He labored on, 'Right from the beginning I knew you were important. That you mattered in some way I couldn't define but that struck me to the heart. I had to take you to the villa, Lucy. I had to. I wanted to forget Lydia and savor you in all your beauty and your passion. But once we'd made love, I knew I was vulnerable again and it scared me blind. I loved you—that's what I realized when I woke with you in my arms in the big bed at the villa. I'd loved my sister and her death had devastated me. And now I was running the same risk again. With you.'

Lucy's eyes widened. 'That's why you couldn't get me out of there fast enough.'

'And then we picked up the deVries family and Shannon walked on board, looking so like Lydia that I could hardly bear it.' He rolled the smooth, heavy piece of glass in his hands, absently watching the colors swirl deep within it. 'I had to shut you out. If I hadn't, I'd have fallen apart.' In a voice so low she could hardly hear it, he added, 'Once they left *Seawind* I went to the villa, and for the first time since Lydia died I wept for her.'

His exhaustion was explained, as was so much else. Trusting her instincts, Lucy closed the distance between them and rested her hands on his taut shoulders. 'And then you came here.'

His muscles were rigid under her palms. 'I should have told you! I know that now and I even knew it at the time. But I'd smothered my grief for my parents' sake, and somehow it got caught. Trapped like a lump of granite in my chest.'

'I do understand, Troy.'

He looked at her, unsmiling. 'I'm sorry for what I put you through. I could see you hurting, but it was as if there was a thick wall between you and me, and I couldn't climb it or breach it. I tried... That was why I was playing one of Lydia's tapes the day I was alone on *Seawind*. But you came back on board before I was ready for you—and I lost my cool and hurt you again.'

Lucy said softly, 'Come to bed with me, Troy. Right now.'

His face stilled. 'If we go to bed, I'll make love to you. Is that what you want?'

'Yes.'

'I don't want an affair with you, Lucy. I want to marry you.'

Her heart skipped a beat. 'Is the wall gone? Or do you think it'll come back?'

'I've learned how to climb it, Lucy. I'm only sorry it took so long.'

She leaned against him, feeling his arms go around her. His body was warm and hard and she hadn't forgotten the smallest detail of their lovemaking. 'I do love you,' she said.

'Marry me, Lucy.'

'Of course,' she said.

Visibly shaken, Troy muttered, 'I was afraid you'd turn me down flat. It would have been no more than I deserve.'

'Troy, it goes without saying that I'll marry you.'

For the first time since she had seen him, waiting on her mother's steps, Troy smiled at her, a smile wry with self-knowledge. 'Nothing goes without saying. That's what I've learned the last few days.' Smoothing a curl back from her forehead, his voice made level with an obvious effort, he said, 'We'll have to figure out how to manage our respective jobs. I'm sure I could get a position in Ottawa...I know how hard you've worked to build up your clientele.'

Touched, Lucy shook her head. 'Thank you for offering. But I think this would be a good time for me to start over, and this time run my business my way and not my family's way. Anyway, we could go sailing on the west coast. It beats the Rideau Canal.'

'I can't believe I'm actually standing here having this conversation,' Troy said huskily. 'Repeat after me—I love you, Troy, and I'll marry you as soon as possible.'

Her smile was dazzling. 'I love you, Troy, and I'll marry you as soon as Catherine gets out of traction. If it hadn't been for her, you wouldn't have known where to find me.'

'I'd have found you,' he said. 'If I'd had to go from door to door through the whole city.'

She believed every word of it. 'Now it's your turn,' she said.

But first he bent his head and kissed her, a kiss that in its intensity told her of his commitment and his hunger and his love. Letting his mouth slide down her throat, he said, 'I love you, Lucy, and we'll get married with Catherine on a stretcher in the aisle.'

'I could have red roses in my bouquet.'

'Only if I can't get hibiscus.'

She laughed. Head to one side, she said, 'Do we have to wait until then to make love?'

His smile had reached his eyes, sparking them with desire. 'We have to wait long enough for me to shower and shave.'

When he'd kissed her his beard had rasped her skin. 'That's a good idea...I could shower with you.'

'Your mother won't walk in? If she's anything like her secretary, I'm already terrified of her.'

'You? Who routed Raymond Blogden? Terrified of my mother?'

'We should invite him to the wedding, too. If it hadn't been for his sexist views on massage, you and I might never have met.'

'I can manage without him,' Lucy said decisively. 'Him and his collection of jade. Although we should ask the Merritts and the Dillons. And you don't have to worry about Mum—she springs from the Puritan work ethic, and won't be home until six-thirty at the earliest.'

Troy looked over at the grandfather clock that was ticking ponderously by the fireplace. 'Five hours. Is that long enough for me to convince you you're the most beautiful woman in the world?'

'You'll never know until you try,' said Lucy.

They made love in her old bedroom, watched benignly by her collection of teddy bears. Passion, hunger and laughter were their bedfellows, and something else, something new to both of them. For this time, openly acknowledged, their love for each other lay between them and enfolded them. Lucy could see it naked in Troy's eyes, and feel it informing each of his caresses. To their mutual climax it gave depth and a fierce poignancy, for in that small death, thought Lucy, was also the first of many beginnings.

They lay for a long time in each other's arms, as Troy recounted some of his memories of his sister. Her veneration for Mozart; her addiction to Pepsi Cola, old Jimmie Stewart movies, and aerobic workouts to improve her wind; the oddly assorted clothing she wore, all secondhand; the single-minded focus she had brought to her music. Lucy wasn't even sure he was aware of the tears in his eyes as he spoke; to her they were beautiful, because they represented truth, and truth was what she needed from this complex and passionate man whom she loved, body and soul.

As if his words had freed him of some of the burden he had been carrying, he slowly started stroking her body, intimately relearning its geography and its responses. Without haste they made love again, a union that was an exploration of all the pleasures of the present as well as a gesture of trust in the future they would share.

It was the distant chiming of the grandfather clock downstairs that brought them back to reality. 'Was that six o'clock?' Lucy gasped.

Troy reached for his watch from the little stand by her bed. 'Yep.' He ran his hands the length of her body. 'You mean I have to get up?'

'I shall refrain from the obvious pun,' Lucy said demurely. 'I suspect my mother is fairly unshockable when it comes to matters of sex—she is a forensic pathologist, after all—but I still don't want her to find me in bed with someone she's never met.'

Troy kissed her firmly and at some length. 'I only hope I brought a clean shirt,' he said, nibbling at her lower lip in a way Lucy found very distracting. 'My mind wasn't on my packing.'

'I'll take you to my favorite Chinese restaurant for dinner,' she said. 'No dress code.'

'You mean your cooking days are over?'

She blinked. 'I forgot to ask you who's skippering *Seawind*!'

'I prevailed upon Gavin to come back with an extra man for crew. Answer the question, Lucy.'

'Not totally over. But I am in favor of take-out. Besides——' and she touched him very suggestively '—I'm not convinced the way to your heart is through your stomach.'

'Stop that! Or we *will* be testing your mother's level of shockability. It's just as well my mother was ahead of her time and taught me how to cook.'

Very reluctantly, Lucy stopped. So, when Evelyn Barnes opened her front door fifteen minutes later, Lucy and Troy were sitting sedately in the den waiting for her.

'Ah,' said Evelyn, after Lucy had introduced him, 'you finally made it here. I rather thought you would.'

Troy kissed Evelyn on the cheek and said, 'I'm hoping you'll become my mother-in-law.'

'A pleasure,' Evelyn said. 'You made it past Margaret and you impressed Catherine, neither of which is a negligible recommendation.' She glanced at her daughter's radiant face. 'And Lucy, I must say, looks happier than I've ever seen her.'

'That,' said Troy, smiling at Lucy, 'is the best recommendation of all.'

The only one that really mattered, thought Lucy, and smiled back.

* * * * *

Meet Troy and Lucy again,
five years into their
marriage...

* * *

Look out for
SECOND HONEYMOON
in August

UNLOCK THE DOOR TO GREAT ROMANCE
AT BRIDE'S BAY RESORT

Join Harlequin's new across-the-lines series, set
in an exclusive hotel on an island off the coast of
South Carolina.

Seven of your favorite authors will bring you exciting stories
about fascinating heroes and heroines discovering love at
Bride's Bay Resort.

Look for these fabulous stories coming to a store near you
beginning in January 1996.

Harlequin American Romance #613 in January
Matchmaking Baby by Cathy Gillen Thacker

Harlequin Presents #1794 in February
Indiscretions by Robyn Donald

Harlequin Intrigue #362 in March
Love and Lies by Dawn Stewardson

Harlequin Romance #3404 in April
Make Believe Engagement by Day Leclaire

Harlequin Temptation #588 in May
Stranger in the Night by Roseanne Williams

Harlequin Superromance #695 in June
Married to a Stranger by Connie Bennett

Harlequin Historicals #324 in July
Dulcie's Gift by Ruth Langan

Visit Bride's Bay Resort each month wherever
Harlequin books are sold.

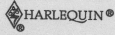

Where there's a will there's a way...
for four charismatic characters to find true love

LANDON'S LEGACY

by Sandra Marton

When Charles Landon dies, he leaves behind a different
legacy for each of his children.

As Cade, Grant, Zach and Kyra react to the terms of
their father's will, each receives an unexpected yet
delightful bequest: a very special love affair
that will last a lifetime.

Coming next month

Book 2: *Guardian Groom*
Harlequin Presents #1813

Grant has been left with the responsibility of acting
as Crista Adams's guardian, and he—who has never
let a woman get under his skin—suddenly finds
himself extremely jealous of every other man in
Crista's life. So Grant decides that Crista must
move in with him—and finds that he keeps *both* eyes
firmly fixed on her! Will life ever be the same again?

Harlequin Presents—you'll want to know what
happens next!

Available in May wherever Harlequin books are sold.

HARLEQUIN PRESENTS®

It's the wedding of the month!

The latest in our tantalizing new selection of stories...

Wedlocked!

Bonded in matrimony, torn by desire...

Coming next month:

THE BRIDE IN BLUE
by Miranda Lee
Harlequin Presents #1811

The author whom everyone's talking about!

It was Sophia's wedding day, but she wasn't a happy and radiant bride. How could she be when she wasn't marrying Godfrey, the father of the baby she was expecting...but his younger brother instead? Jonathon Parnell was ruthlessly carrying out the deathbed promise he's made to Godfrey: to marry Sophia and look after their child. Jonathon claimed he wanted Sophia only as a wife of convenience, but Sophia suspected that, actually, Jonathon wanted *her*...

Available in May wherever Harlequin books are sold.

Fall in love all over again with

This Time... MARRIAGE

In this collection of original short stories, three brides get a unique chance for a return engagement!

- Being kidnapped from your bridal shower by a one-time love can really put a crimp in your wedding plans! *The Borrowed Bride*— by **Susan Wiggs**, *Romantic Times* Career Achievement Award-winning author.

- After fifteen years a couple reunites for the sake of their child—this time will it end in marriage? *The Forgotten Bride*—by **Janice Kaiser**.

- It's tough to make a good divorce stick—especially when you're thrown together with your ex in a magazine wedding shoot! *The Bygone Bride*— by **Muriel Jensen**.

Don't miss THIS TIME...MARRIAGE, available in April wherever Harlequin books are sold.

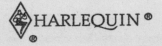
HARLEQUIN ®
®

BRIDE96